"What are you doing in my bedroom?"

"I'm seducing you," Cody said.

Serena shook her head. "I'm supposed to do that to you."

He laughed; she was drunker than he'd thought. But then he remembered her friend's crazy suggestion. "That's right. You're supposed to seduce *me*."

"I don't want to talk..." She reached up and locked her arms around his neck, then she pulled him down on top of her. "I just want you." Her lips parted as she kissed him.

His body ached for hers. He wanted her so badly. But not like this. He pulled back. "Serena..."

She was definitely awake now, her hands tugging at his shirt and then his belt. Before he could stop her, she pulled it free. The buckle hit the floor with a clank, and she giggled. Then she reached for the button at his waist. He sucked in a breath as her fingers dipped inside.

Did he have the willpower to control his desire?

Dear Reader,

I hope you've been enjoying my Hotshot Heroes series! I've been having so much fun writing stories for these sexy firefighters. Wyatt and Dawson weren't just fighting fires or even their attraction to the women they knew would change their lives. They had to deal with the relentless teasing of their good friend and fellow Hotshot Cody Mallehan.

I have to confess that Cody is my favorite Hotshot. He's such a flirt. But when I started writing his book, Cody surprised me more than any character has in a long time. I can understand how Serena Beaumont has such a struggle resisting his charms. I hope you enjoy his story as much as I loved writing it.

Happy reading!

Lisa Childs

Lisa Childs

———

Hot Seduction

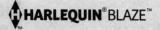

Recycling programs
for this product may
not exist in your area.

ISBN-13: 978-0-373-79913-8

Hot Seduction

Copyright © 2016 by Lisa Childs

Printed in U.S.A.

www.Harlequin.com

Ever since **Lisa Childs** read her first romance novel
(a Harlequin story, of course) at age eleven, all she
wanted was to be a romance writer. With over forty
novels published with Harlequin, Lisa is living her dream.
She is an award-winning, bestselling romance author.
Lisa loves to hear from readers, who can contact her on
Facebook, through her website, lisachilds.com, or her
snail-mail address, PO Box 139, Marne, MI 49435.

Books by Lisa Childs

Harlequin Blaze

Hotshot Heroes

Red Hot
Hot Attraction

Harlequin Romantic Suspense

Bachelor Bodyguards

His Christmas Assignment
Bodyguard Daddy
Bodyguard's Baby Surprise
Beauty and the Bodyguard

Harlequin Intrigue

Special Agents at the Altar

The Pregnant Witness
Agent Undercover
The Agent's Redemption

Shotgun Weddings

Groom Under Fire
Explosive Engagement
Bridegroom Bodyguard

To get the inside scoop on Harlequin Blaze and its talented
writers, be sure to check out blazeauthors.com.

All backlist available in ebook format.

Visit the Author Profile page at
Harlequin.com for more titles.

With great love and appreciation to Andrew Ahearne for believing in and supporting me.

1

Hot breath caressed his skin as someone panted in Cody Mallehan's ear. Then a wet, warm tongue slid over his naked shoulder. He shivered and shifted on the stiff firehouse cot. His body tensed. He hadn't brought anyone back to the firehouse with him the night before. He had never done that, so he had to be dreaming.

The tongue moved to his face now, slobbering all over him. He cursed and opened his eyes and met the adoring gaze of a besotted female. Too bad she was a bitch.

He pushed off the oversize puppy. She was some kind of mixed breed of big dog and even bigger dog. Maybe an English sheepdog and a mastiff because her black-and-gray hair was long and so were her drooling jowls. With the back of his hand, he wiped her doggy slobber off his face. His stubble, which always came in darker than his blond hair, scraped the skin of his hand. He needed to shave. And after the doggy tongue bath, he definitely needed to shower, too.

"Annie, what the hell are you doing here?" he wondered aloud.

Someone had abandoned the mutt at the firehouse a few weeks ago. But Stanley—the kid that Cody had convinced the superintendent to hire to do odd jobs around the house—was supposed to have delivered her to the humane society.

A chuckle—too deep to be Stanley's—echoed off the cement-block walls of the bunkroom. As far as Cody knew, he was the only one who'd been crashing at the firehouse. He sat up and looked around and discovered his boss kneeling just inside the doorway as Annie jumped all over him.

"It's not like you to turn away a female's attention," Superintendent Braden Zimmer said. His eyes, which were the same brown as his hair, twinkled with amusement.

Cody grinned. He liked seeing the other man like this—joking around again—instead of all depressed over his divorce. So he didn't correct him. Everybody had the impression that Cody was some big player. Okay, maybe that was because he worked hard to give that impression. But he didn't even date during wildfire season—unlike some of his fellow Hotshots who'd recently fallen in love.

Hotshots were the US Forest Service's elite firefighters. During the off-season, they were regular firefighters, working out of firehouses all over the region. Cody worked out of the village of Northern Lakes, Michigan. He was in Northern Lakes now even though it wasn't the off-season. There had already been a couple of huge blazes here in the Huron National Forest. And it was probable that there would be another… Unless they caught the person who had been setting the fires.

No, Cody was too focused on the job to date, especially now with an arsonist preying on the town. He couldn't afford any distractions. And he had never allowed himself any entanglements.

"You must be having a dry spell," Superintendent Zimmer continued.

Maybe he hadn't been working hard enough on his womanizing image. Or maybe he'd been with the Huron Hotshots long enough that they were getting to know the real him. This was his second season with them, and two years was longer than he'd stayed anywhere. His blood chilling, he shivered with dread. He didn't want anyone to know the *real* him. "What makes you say that?"

"Since your cabin burned down, you've been sleeping in the firehouse instead of some woman's bed."

"I never *sleep* in some woman's bed," he quipped cockily.

"That's because he's worried her husband will catch him," another deep voice chimed in as Wyatt Andrews stepped into the bunkroom. His black hair was all slicked back with sweat; he must have just finished a workout in the weight room. "Cody only goes after other guys' women."

He only flirted with them because he knew it was safe. He knew there was no risk—beyond getting his ass kicked. He could handle the physical pain. It was the emotional pain he avoided at all costs. A split lip or a black eye hurt a hell of a lot less than someone letting him down.

Cody grinned. "Getting nervous?" he asked Wyatt. "There's still time for your fiancée to realize I'm the better man."

Wyatt snorted. He had every confidence—and with good reason—that Fiona O'Brien would become his bride. Their wedding wasn't until the wildfire season was over, though. The only thing that might thwart their plans was the arsonist. They needed to catch him.

Cody wiped sleep and the rest of the dog's slobber from his eyes, and peered at the clock on the wall behind Wyatt's sweaty head. Had he slept late?

"Why are you guys here already?" he asked. "The team meeting isn't for a few hours yet." Adrenaline coursed through his body. If there was a local fire, he would have heard the alarm. No matter how tired he was, he couldn't sleep through that ear-piercing siren. So they had to be getting called out to a wildfire.

He lived for this—for the travel, for the adventure, for the excitement and most especially for the triumph when they extinguished the blaze. All those things were why he had become a Hotshot. And the fact that he'd needed a couple of years of experience as a Hotshot before he could get a position as a smoke jumper.

That job involved even more travel and adventure and danger.

"Where are we going?" he excitedly asked. "Washington? California?"

Wildfires had been raging out west for a while. They'd already done a couple of week-long stints on the front lines of each of those blazes, cutting breaks—trying to contain the beast. By removing all the vegetation, they starved the fire of fuel, until it eventually burned itself out.

The hard work burned out a lot of Hotshots, too. They were probably needed to relieve another team.

Braden shook his head. "No, I passed on this assignment."

They had been called up and Superintendent Zimmer had refused to go?

Cody cursed—because he knew why. "That damn arsonist." That was undoubtedly why Braden had called the whole team together for a meeting later that day. But that didn't explain why Braden and Wyatt had come in to the firehouse so early.

"Why are you two here now?"

"Because of you," Wyatt replied.

"What about me?" Cody asked as his blood chilled again. The air was blasting in the firehouse, and the cement-block walls kept it cool. But that wasn't why he was cold.

Wyatt Andrews was one of Zimmer's two assistants. In addition to his duties at a fire, he also helped Braden with personnel issues.

Did they have a problem with him—with his work?

Sure, he was a smart-ass most of the time. But he was also damn serious about his job. It meant everything to him; he had nothing else.

"Let's go to the Filling Station," Zimmer suggested.

Did his boss think he would need a drink to swallow whatever they had to tell him? Or that it was better to tell him in a public place so that he wouldn't make a scene?

"It's too early to drink," Cody said. He really wasn't the wild guy he pretended to be. Didn't they realize that? That was the drawback to never letting anyone get too close, though. But he would prefer that they not really know him rather than know him too well. He didn't need their pity.

Zimmer chuckled again. "They serve coffee, too, you know. You look like you could use some."

He hadn't been out the night before. "I'm not hungover," he protested.

Wyatt snorted now—derisively. "So you look like hell for no reason."

"He looks like hell because he's been crashing here since his cabin burned down," Braden said. "These bunks are miserable to sleep on."

"Maybe the firehouse superintendent should order some new ones," Cody suggested.

Braden mock-glared at him. "You need to find a real bed."

"You need a place to stay," Wyatt said. "You can't stay here."

Cody chuckled, albeit a little nervously. "What is this? An intervention?"

"Sort of," Braden admitted. "The US Forest Service has decided not to rebuild your cabin, at least not until we've caught the arsonist."

"Of course." The son of a bitch kept restarting fires on the scorched ground he'd already burned. The only good thing about this was that there wasn't enough fuel left to keep the fire burning. Usually the hay bales he poured gasoline over burned out quickly, and the fire didn't spread. But occasionally the guy started new areas of the forest on fire—like he had when he'd torched the woods where Cody's cabin had been.

"You need to relocate," Wyatt said.

He could have laughed again, but it would have had a bitter ring to it. He'd been told so many times that he needed to move—that he wasn't welcome anymore.

"You kicking me off the team?" he asked. And he was surprised that his voice didn't crack with the emotion that overwhelmed him. But he wasn't a kid anymore. He could take care of himself; he had for years.

"Of course not," Braden said. "We're kicking you off the cot."

"We all offered you a bed," Wyatt reminded him. "You can crash at any one of our places."

Until he inevitably wore out his welcome.

"You don't get enough of me now?" he teased.

"I'm usually not there," Wyatt said. "I stay at Fiona's."

Or she stayed at his place. Despite Cody's teasing, he didn't want to interfere in his friend's relationship. The Hotshots were sometimes gone for weeks at a time, so they needed to spend as much time as they could with their loved ones when they were in town. That was why he had also refused to stay with Dawson Hess, Zimmer's other assistant. Cody hadn't wanted to put a crimp in his new relationship with the hot reporter, Avery Kincaid.

"Don't worry about me," he said. "Last night was my last night here. I found a place." He actually didn't want to stay *there*, but now he had no choice. He just hoped like hell he was better at avoiding temptation than his teammates.

HER HAND SHAKING, Serena Beaumont set the court order on her desk next to her mother's portrait. She blinked back tears, so that she could focus on the picture. She had been told—many times—that she looked like her mother. Sure, she had the same long black hair and dark eyes. But she felt the resemblance ended there. She didn't have Priscilla's delicate features or the inner beauty that radiated from the portrait. Nor did she have her mother's strength.

She was about to lose the family home that her mother had fought so hard to keep—so hard that it had probably led to the heart attack that had taken her too soon a year ago.

Serena drew in a deep, albeit shaky, breath and lifted her chin. She wasn't giving up yet. Sure, it was a lot of money. But she didn't have to sell the house. She only had to come up with half the value of it.

A year ago she'd been turned down for a loan. But that had been before she'd gotten more boarders in the house. Now she could show that the property could support itself. Or it would...

If she could rent out the rest of the rooms...

Only four of the eight bedrooms were rented. In order to show any kind of profit, she needed to fill the house—like it had been filled when she was little.

When the sweet-talking man who had gotten her pregnant abandoned her, Priscilla Beaumont had become a single mom to her twin daughters. But she hadn't raised Serena and Courtney alone. She'd had Grandma's help. They had lived in this house with their grandmother, an aunt, an uncle and some cousins. Serena was the only member of the Beaumont family left in the house now. She was the only one who cared about her heritage—about how her great-great-grandfather, a French trapper, had settled down near the village of Northern Lakes and built this house for his Native American bride.

Two and a half stories with a double-decker wraparound porch, the plantation-style house had also served as a stagecoach stop, although coaches hadn't often passed through this remote area of Michigan. Adjoining the Huron National Forest, the house was still miles from the village of Northern Lakes. Maybe that was why it was hard for her to find boarders. Most people would rather live in town.

Serena loved the house and the property. She'd already come close to losing it, but the local Hotshot crew had stopped the fire before it had consumed more than the acres of forest that were now just scorched black earth.

She and the house had survived then. They would again. Somehow…

She drew in another breath, but this one was steadier. It wasn't just her anxiety making it harder for her to breathe; it was the stifling heat. Sweat trickled down the back of her neck, beneath the thick fall of hair.

If she were to get any more boarders, she would need to fix the air conditioning unit. It had been broken for a few weeks. Mrs. Gulliver and Mr. Stehouwer didn't mind; the heat didn't bother the octogenarians. Mr. Tremont was younger than them—probably only in his forties or early fifties. But he wasn't home much. Neither was Stanley, and when the teenager was here, he was usually outside—like he was now.

The kid lounged on the wide front porch. She could see him through the window of her office, which had formerly been the front parlor since its burled oak pocket doors opened onto the wide foyer. Those doors were open, and so was the heavy front door and every window, but no breeze blew through the house.

The air was so still that the sound of an engine startled her. She glanced out the window but could see only the grill of a truck as it pulled up to the house. Then she heard Stanley call out, "Hey, Cody!"

Her pulse quickened more than it had when she'd opened the thick envelope from the lawyer's office. Then her heart had raced with fear; now, it pounded with excitement.

Just looking at Cody Mallehan was exciting. With his blond hair, clear green eyes, and muscular build he was beyond handsome. He was probably also bad news for a woman like her.

He was a player. Or so her friends had warned her. The few times she'd seen him before today he hadn't flirted with her, though. Of course, they'd talked business then because he'd brought Stanley as a boarder.

One truck door slammed. Then another opened. Maybe he was bringing someone else to rent a room.

She glanced at her mother's portrait. Mama would

have cautioned her to stay away from a man like her father, who was only passing through. Everyone said that Cody Mallehan grew bored quickly—with women and locations. He wouldn't be sticking around.

That was good, though. Serena didn't need him; she just needed the business he brought her. She was too smart to fall for a man like him anyway. She was in no danger of losing her heart; Serena's only concern was that she not lose her house.

2

CODY WAS GLAD that he saw Stanley first—sitting on the porch swing of Serena Beaumont's ridiculously large, yellow-clapboard house. He'd lived in group homes that had been smaller than her place. It was a great boardinghouse.

Not that she had many boarders. The last time he'd stopped by, she'd just had a couple of old folks and Stanley. Probably because it was too far from town. The house was slightly closer than his cabin had been, but the long drive had still given Annie enough time to lick him nearly half to death. He should have made the dog ride in the pickup bed.

"Out!" he told her, pointing at the ground. Finally she leaped down from the passenger's seat.

"Annie!" Stanley exclaimed with joy. He dropped to his knees and embraced the mutt who jumped all over him, licking his face.

"Don't act so surprised to see her," Cody said. "You're the one who brought her back to the firehouse—after I told you to take her to the humane society."

"I did," Stanley replied, quickly and defensively, "when you told me to."

"That was weeks ago," Cody said. He narrowed his eyes and studied the curly-haired kid's face, which was wet with dog drool. Skeptically, he asked, "So what did she do? Break out and find her own way back?"

The dog hadn't been able to find her own way to the ground from his pickup. He doubted she'd been able to track her way back to the firehouse. Bloodhound was probably the only breed not in her family tree.

"No…" Stanley reluctantly admitted. "I broke her out."

"Why?"

"Because her time was almost up," Stanley said.

"What do you mean?" But Cody was afraid that he knew. As if sensing his distress, Annie turned her attention from the kid back to him. She bounded down the porch steps and jumped up on him. Her jowly face and almost soulful brown eyes nearly on the same level as his, she stared at Cody. He pushed her huge paws off his chest, but then patted her head gently.

"They only keep the animals for so long. Then, if nobody adopts them, they put them down, Cody," Stanley slowly explained—as if he were the adult and Cody the kid who didn't understand. The eighteen-year-old's voice cracked when he added, "If they did the same thing with people…"

Cody and Stanley would have been dead long ago, since they'd spent most of their lives in foster homes. That was how they'd met. Cody had been forced to leave their group home when he turned eighteen, but he'd kept in touch with Stanley.

Cody had been adopted once, but adopting him had put a strain on the young couple's marriage, and after a few years they had returned him to the system—like someone might a dog to the pound. He'd been so young that he didn't even remember them.

Stanley had been born premature and addicted to crack, so no one had been willing to take a chance on a child who might have lifelong physical and mental disabilities. That was probably why Stanley felt such a kinship with the dog.

Annie whined and pushed her head harder against Cody's hand. He had a kinship with the damn dog, too. The puppy had been abandoned at the firehouse—just as he had been abandoned as an infant at a firehouse in Detroit. The guys had named her Orphan Annie.

"That sucks," Cody agreed. "But I don't know where we're going to keep her."

"We're going to keep her?" Stanley asked, his brown eyes wide with hope.

Cody knew better than to make any promises. "I don't know if we can…" He didn't have a place to stay himself, let alone room for a dog. Unless…

As if Stanley had guessed what Cody was thinking, he said, "Miss Serena already told me Annie can't stay here 'cause she's not housebroken."

"Is that why you brought her to the firehouse?"

The kid nodded, and some blond curls fell into his face. He really needed a haircut; Cody would have to bring him by the barber. "Yeah…"

"She can't stay there either," he said. "She peed in Superintendent Zimmer's office."

Stanley's brown eyes widened. "How mad was he?"

Braden had actually laughed. But he'd also told Cody to take the dog with him when he left. "I don't think she'll be welcome there again."

"But if we have no place to keep her…" Stanley's voice cracked with emotion. "And we bring her back to the humane society…"

"Maybe she'll be adopted this time," Cody said.

Stanley shook his head. "She's too big. Nobody wants a dog that big, they said." His brown eyes filled with tears.

"She can stay."

Cody's body tensed at the sound of the husky, female voice. He braced himself before turning to where Serena had stepped out onto the porch. She was so damn beautiful. Ever since the first moment he'd met her, he'd been having fantasies about her long, thick hair—about tangling his fingers in it, about…

His mind went blank as his gaze focused on her. It was so hot that he shouldn't have been surprised she was wearing shorts. But he hadn't pictured her as the type to wear cutoff Daisy Dukes, and he'd pictured her in a lot of different things—and nothing at all—since he'd met her. Her legs were long and tanned or maybe that was just the natural hue of her honey-toned skin. With the cutoffs, she wore a pale pink tank top, probably in deference to the heat. Her hair was down, reaching nearly to her narrow waist.

"Annie can stay?" Stanley asked hopefully.

Cody was surprised the kid had enough wits about him to pose a question. His tongue was tied. But she had that effect on him. She was the first woman he'd met that he hadn't been able to flirt with.

"She can stay outside and in the enclosed porches," Serena allowed. "I don't want her peeing in my house. Or chewing up any of my great-grandmother's antiques."

Stanley nodded. "Yes, ma'am."

Ma'am? Cody winced. He was twenty-seven and didn't like to be called "sir" yet. Serena had to be a few years younger than he was—way too young to be called "ma'am."

"You should get her some water now," Serena told Stanley. "With all that hair, she must be overheated." As she said it, she lifted her own hair from the back of her neck. Her face was flushed; she was hot, too.

So hot…

And sexy…

Nearly tripping over his feet in his anxiousness to obey her—or maybe to please her—Stanley hurried into the house.

Cody could understand wanting to please her. He'd like to try himself. As all the naked images popped into his head, his throat thickened with desire. He cleared it to say, "Thank you."

Serena nodded.

"What about me?" he asked, even though he knew it was a bad idea. "Can I stay, too?"

Her dark eyes widened in surprise.

He should have asked her for a room weeks ago instead of crashing at the firehouse. But with the arsonist on the loose, he'd thought it was smart to stay close— and there wasn't any place closer than the house itself. When those hot spots had flared up again with the arsonist's help, he'd been the first one ready to go.

But the guys wanted him to have a softer bed so he could get more rest. When they were on the job—sometimes for weeks at a time—they got very little sleep.

Another reason he'd decided to crash at the firehouse instead of getting a room here was because of Serena, though. He wasn't sure how much sleep he would actually get with her so temptingly close.

Her lips parted, but she said nothing—her hesitation obvious. She didn't seem to want him in her house any more than she wanted the dog.

So he promised her, "I won't pee in your house or chew up your great-grandmother's antiques."

She hesitated another long moment before replying, "Then I guess you can stay."

WHAT THE HELL had she been thinking?

Sure, she needed more tenants to be able to show the bank that the boardinghouse could be a profitable business. She'd even hoped that Cody was bringing her another boarder. She hadn't thought *he* would be that boarder, though.

Grandma would've said it was like letting a fox into the hen house. Of course, she and Mrs. Gulliver were the only hens. And Mrs. Gulliver was eighty-six.

And despite all the things Serena had heard about Cody Mallehan being a shameless womanizer, he hadn't really even flirted with her. Of course she wasn't his type. Guys like him loved fun-loving, lighthearted women. She was too serious for him, too stressed thanks to that damn lawsuit. She also didn't care about makeup and clothes, about dressing to attract men.

Not that she didn't want a man. But she didn't want just any man; she wanted one who was as serious as she was—who would stay and help her raise a family someday in this house. That was why she couldn't lose it.

She had too many hopes and dreams for it—for someday filling it with family, like Grandma had.

No, she definitely wasn't Cody's type any more than he was hers. But as she climbed the staircase ahead of him, his gaze was on her ass. She doubted she was just imagining it because it was so palpable she could almost feel it. The elaborate polished oak staircase was extra wide; he could have walked beside her, like a gentleman, but he was taking the opportunity to ogle her instead.

Settling in a boarder was her job, not another tenant's, or she would have had Stanley show Cody to his room. They would both be on the second floor. Fortunately, her room was not; she lived in the attic, which had been converted to a studio apartment long ago.

As she reached the second-floor landing, she expelled a shaky breath of relief. She was almost there. But a strong hand closed around her wrist, stopping her. Her skin tingled beneath his touch.

"What's up there?" Cody gestured toward the narrower flight of stairs that led to the third floor.

"My private quarters," she said. She had no intention

of ever letting him up to the small space dominated by her great-grandmother's old brass bed.

She tugged free of his grasp and headed down the hall toward the room at the end. As Cody followed, she hurried past all the six panel mahogany doors. As she passed an open one, she pointed. "There's the bathroom. There are two on this floor. One on this side of the stairwell and one on the other side."

He nodded but he didn't even glance inside the room—which was good since she still needed to clean it. His gaze remained on her; it was so intense that her hand shook as she reached for the doorknob for his room.

"And this is where you'll be staying."

She had put him in the biggest second-floor room, which was also the most masculine with its mahogany trim, dark stained wood floor, and navy blue walls. She stepped back to let him pass her. But he brushed against her anyway, his chest and hip bumping into hers.

Something flared in his green eyes. Or maybe it had already been there—an intensity that unnerved her. As she held out the room key to him, her hand shook so much that she dropped it. He leaned down to pick it up, and his soft hair whispered across her bare legs.

Despite the heat, she shivered. "I should have opened the window," she murmured and hurried over to it. She needed the air. More than that, she needed the distance from him. But even though it was the biggest bedroom, it wasn't big enough for her to escape his presence.

She threw up the sash, but no breeze blew in through the window. Not a tree limb or leaf moved in the woods that surrounded the house. She drew in a deep breath and turned back toward Cody.

Now he was leaning over the duffel bag he'd dropped onto the red-and-blue plaid bedspread. His jeans were faded and so worn at the seams that she caught glimpses of blue underwear through the thin material.

Sweat trickled down between her shoulder blades. He was so damn sexy. It wasn't fair.

"I'm sorry," she murmured.

He glanced up in surprise. "What are you sorry about? The room is great."

She was sorry about the air. But since he hadn't mentioned it, she didn't either. She gestured toward his duffel bag. "I'm sorry your cabin burned down."

"You didn't do it," he said. His eyes narrowed, but a grin curved up the corners of his mouth. "Unless you're confessing to being the arsonist…"

She uttered a kind of you-caught-me sigh. "If I was, I'd be pretty stupid letting a fireman move in." Her decision had been stupid, though, because she was already under enough stress. Now she had to fight her attraction to him, too.

"I'm sorry that you lost everything in that fire," she clarified.

He chuckled. "I didn't have much to lose," he said. "I travel light—because I travel often."

Was he warning her? He needn't have bothered. Her friends had already done that. They'd thought he might ask to stay at her boardinghouse when his cabin had burned down.

"Well, I'll leave you to unpack," she said.

"I usually don't bother," he told her.

Of course he wouldn't be staying long. So she would have to apply for that loan quickly—before he left. "I'll be in the office if you need me," she murmured as she hurried for the door.

She doubted he would need her. So she settled back into her office with a glass of iced tea. She fished an ice cube from the glass and pressed it to her throat. She could almost feel it sizzle against her hot skin. She would like to blame the lack of air-conditioning for why she was so overheated. But she suspected that wasn't the only reason now—not with Cody Mallehan moving in.

Knuckles rapped against wood, startling her. She dropped the ice cube, which slid down her neck to disappear between her breasts.

She glanced up to find Cody leaning against the frame of the pocket door to her office. Hopefully he was on his way out.

"Want me to get that for you?" he asked, his mouth curving into a wicked grin. *Now* he was flirting with her?

Had he refrained earlier so that she would let him move in? Serena could still ask him to leave, if it got too uncomfortable—more uncomfortable than the ice cube melting in her cleavage.

Her brain muddled, she could only murmur, "It's hot…"

Hotter now that he was here. His green eyes twinkled with amusement—and something else—as he studied the wet trail the cube left on the front of her shirt.

"It's damn hot," he agreed.

Maybe it was because of the way he was staring—or maybe it was because of the ice cube—but her nipples tightened inside her lacy bra and pushed against the thin material of her tank top.

"I have a repairman coming out to fix the air-conditioning," she said.

Or she would have the technician come out, as soon as she came up with enough money for the service call and whatever else he might charge to get the old unit functioning again. But she didn't want Cody to know that; she couldn't afford to lose a renter, especially now.

And that was why she had to ignore the attraction she felt for him. A man like Cody wouldn't stay in the home of a woman he'd slept with. He was definitely the love 'em and leave 'em type. That part of the rumors she'd heard was true, she knew—or he wouldn't be renting a room from her. He'd be living with one of his lovers.

"I didn't realize the air was out," he said. And that wicked grin widened.

He was definitely flirting with her. Her pulse quickened. He shouldn't be flirting.

But then he probably didn't care if he stayed in her house or not. Eventually the US Forest Service would rebuild his cabin. Or he'd go back to staying in the firehouse where she'd heard he'd been sleeping since the last fire.

Remembering how the flames and smoke had painted the sky red and black over Northern Lakes, she shuddered. The fire had come too close to the house—licking at the trees at the edge of her property.

"I thought you were hot," he said. "But now you're shivering."

She sighed. "I was just thinking about the arsonist—how he could strike again at any time…" Which was another good reason to have a firefighter living in her house.

The flirty sparkle of amusement left his green eyes, leaving them dark and hard. His voice gruff with emotion and determination, he said, "We are going to catch him."

She nodded. "I know."

He released a ragged breath. "That's where I'm heading now. The whole Hotshot team is having a meeting at the firehouse. I just popped in to your office to give you this," he said. His long strides closed the distance between them in two steps. He dropped a wad of cash on the desk. "This is my rent," he said. "And the other amount we agreed on…"

For months he had secretly been paying half of Stanley's room and board. A lot of people talked about Cody—about his skirt-chasing, about his bar-brawling, about his risk-taking—but nobody talked about his generosity. Because they didn't know.

Only she knew that there was more to Cody than the rumors swirling around Northern Lakes, and that made him even more attractive to her. She glanced down at the cash; there was enough to get the air fixed now, even if the condenser was beyond repair like the serviceman had already warned her.

"Thank you," she murmured. She should have been relieved, but there was an emptiness inside her. While it was enough money to fix the air-conditioning, it wasn't enough to satisfy the lawsuit. She needed more if she was going to have any hope of keeping her family heritage.

He leaned over her desk, so close that his face nearly touched hers as he murmured in her ear, "And remember—"

Remember? What was she supposed to remember? With him so close she could barely think.

"—this is between you and me." His breath caressed the side of her face, making her skin tingle. "Stanley can't ever know."

Cody had brought Stanley to her boardinghouse when the kid had turned eighteen and lost his eligibility to stay in foster care. She wasn't sure how he even knew the kid or why he cared. But he did—obviously a lot.

She shook her head, but he hadn't moved his. Their mouths nearly touched. She drew in a shaky breath and assured him, "I haven't told anyone."

"It's our little secret then," he said. The amusement was back, glinting in his green eyes. He didn't straighten up and move away. Instead he leaned closer.

She could feel the heat of his breath on her lips now. Her lashes fluttered in anticipation of his mouth moving over hers. He was going to kiss her.

But then an alarm rang out. He jerked away from her as he pulled his cell phone from his pocket. He cursed.

"There's a fire?"

He spared her only a quick nod before turning to rush out the door. She hoped the arsonist hadn't struck again; the last fire he'd started had been too close.

Hopefully something else had caused a fire. Lightning. Bad wiring. An overheated car.

Or Cody Mallehan.

Because she was pretty sure he'd started a fire inside her. Her fingers trembling, she fished out another ice cube. She could dump the whole glass down her tank top, but she doubted it would cool the desire she felt for her new boarder.

3

CODY HAD PUT OUT one fire with the extinguisher he carried in his truck. But there was another fire he couldn't put out. The one burning between him and his hot landlady…

If the fire alarm on his phone hadn't rung, he might have done something really stupid. He might have kissed her. Their mouths had been so close that he'd almost tasted the sugar on her lips from her glass of sweet tea. Remembering the trail the ice cube had taken from her throat, over the swell of her breast to disappear in her cleavage, he groaned.

"What's the matter with you?" Dawson Hess asked. The dark-haired guy sat next to Cody in the big conference room on the third floor of the firehouse.

"What do you mean?" he asked.

"That groan is the first sound I've heard you make since you rolled in here late," Dawson said.

During the meeting Cody had managed to hold in his disappointment that they still had no leads on the arsonist. But that was just about all he remembered of the meeting.

"You're never quiet," Wyatt chimed in from the other side of Dawson. His blue gaze held some concern. "What's wrong?"

Owen James leaned forward from the chairs behind them and asked, "Something's wrong?"

In addition to being a Hotshot, the former army medic was an emergency medical tech for Northern Lakes during the off-season. Like the rest of them, he'd no doubt been stationed at home again because of the arsonist. So far nobody had been seriously hurt in any of the fires.

But the arsonist was getting more and more dangerous. It would only be a matter of time—unless they stopped him.

Cody shook his head and reassured them all. He forced his usual cocky grin. "Just getting sick of doing all the work around here."

Concern gone, Wyatt snorted—which Owen echoed.

"Hey, I had to put out a car fire on my way in," Cody said. "That's why I was late."

"That fire was on M87," Owen said. "What were you doing out there?"

"I'm staying out that way," Cody replied.

"At the Beaumont boardinghouse?" Wyatt asked. He nodded.

Wyatt snorted again. "That's not going to last."

"Why not?"

"Serena Beaumont isn't going to put up with you hitting on her," Wyatt said. "She's like Fiona used to be."

"She thinks getting involved with a firefighter is too great a risk because of our dangerous jobs?" As an insurance agent, Fiona O'Brien had statistics to back up her belief. Unfortunately, the wildfires burning out west had added to those statistics when a few more firefighters had lost their lives battling those blazes. The Huron Hotshots had spent a few weeks helping out there, but their greatest threat was at home.

Wyatt shrugged. "Serena is Fiona's friend. But I don't know her really well. Since her mom died last year, she's been busy trying to run that boardinghouse all by herself."

With the size of the place, Cody could understand how just cleaning it would keep her busy. But cooking and caring for people, too?

That was why he preferred to live alone now that he had a choice. He'd loved his cabin out in the middle of nowhere. Then, he hadn't had to put up with, or take care of, anyone else. Sure, it had been too quiet sometimes. But that was just because he was used to noise, used to people being around.

It didn't mean that he hated being alone. Or that he got lonely...

A person could be lonely even living in a house full of people. Was Serena lonely?

Something seemed to have been bothering her earlier. She'd looked upset or sad. But maybe she still missed her mom. Cody wouldn't know what that might be like. You couldn't miss what you'd never had.

"So you're saying she doesn't have any time to put up with Cody's flirty bullshit," Dawson summed up for Wyatt.

But she'd given Cody her time. She hadn't thrown

him out of her office when he'd flirted with her earlier. She hadn't pulled away when he'd leaned in close.

Her thick lashes had fluttered, and she had closed her big, dark eyes as if anticipating his kiss. His stomach muscles tightened; he'd wanted to kiss her, to taste her...

But it was better that he hadn't. "I didn't know that she lost her mom last year." All he'd known was that she owned a huge house and was damn hot.

Dawson nodded. "Owen and I went out on the call." If he wasn't too busy with his assistant superintendent duties, Dawson occasionally helped out at as paramedic.

"She died right in that house," Owen added with a soft sigh. "We got there as quickly as we could, but we were too late to save her. Serena had tried—unsuccessfully—to resuscitate her until we got there."

Cody cursed. He remembered that frustration of being unable to save someone. He'd been just a kid when he'd watched a person die for the first time. The boy had been in the same foster home as Cody, but not for long. Nobody had been warned of the five-year-old's peanut allergy—until it had been too late to save him. The home had been shut down after his death and Cody moved to another one.

"She's been through a lot," Owen said sympathetically, as if that EMT call still bothered him.

All of the Hotshots worked in other capacities in the off-season. Wyatt and Braden manned the Northern Lakes firehouse. Cody worked as a US Forest Service ranger and backup for the firehouse. Dawson also worked as a backup firefighter and backup EMT. Owen worked primarily as an EMT and usually ran out of the hospital some forty-five minutes north of Northern Lakes.

Wyatt leaned closer and warned Cody, "So don't mess with her."

Cody hated messes and getting involved with his landlady would definitely lead to one. He nodded his agreement, but then that vision of the ice cube sliding down into her cleavage flashed behind his eyes.

"As soon as Avery's place is rebuilt, you can take my cabin," Dawson offered.

"You're moving in with her?" Cody asked. He had never lived with anyone before—at least, not just one person. There had usually been several other kids in those foster homes, especially the group ones he'd lived in when he'd gotten older.

Dawson grinned. "Not that she'll be home much with her new job."

After breaking the story of the arsonist attacking Northern Lakes, the reporter had received more attention than the culprit, which had led to an impressive new career opportunity for her.

"Has the arsonist tried to contact her again?" Cody asked.

Dawson's brow furrowed. "I already answered that question during the meeting."

"I must have missed that part…" Because he'd been thinking about that damn ice cube with an envy he'd never felt before. Of course, he'd been preoccupied with Serena since he'd brought Stanley out to live with her. For the past few months he'd been having erotic dreams about her. He'd been obsessed with images of her long, silky hair—of only her hair covering the sweet curves of her naked body.

"You were sitting right next to me," Dawson pointed out. He stared intently at Cody, as if trying to figure out what was going on with him.

He didn't know himself. While he enjoyed women, he had never let one distract him from his job before. Unnerved, he forced some more cockiness into his voice to cover it up. "You know I don't listen unless I'm the one talking."

Wyatt chuckled. "Ain't that the truth."

Dawson didn't seem to buy the explanation as easily. But he answered Cody's question. "No, the arsonist hasn't contacted her." He sounded relieved.

But they could have used another lead. Any lead…

"This must be killing you," Ethan Sommerly commented as he dropped onto the chair next to Owen and right behind Cody.

Dawson turned fully around and said, "We all want the arsonist caught."

"I know that," Ethan said. "I was talking about Mallehan having to stick around Northern Lakes in case the arsonist decides to strike again." His huge hand grabbed Cody's shoulder. "It has to be killing you to stay in one place."

Ethan was a ranger, too—in a vast national forest in the upper peninsula. He actually enjoyed living in the middle of nowhere and nothing, which Cody had often needled him about. With his bushy beard and long hair, the guy looked like a mountain man.

Cody grinned and faked a shudder. "You know me."

Everybody thought they did. And Cody would have agreed with them until now. Now—with thoughts of a woman distracting him from the job that meant everything to him—he wasn't even sure he knew himself.

"Do you have a strong lock for your bedroom door?" Serena's insurance agent asked.

"I have dead bolts on all the doors," Serena replied. "You know that. I thought you were already giving me a discount." Not that she used them… She didn't want to lock out a boarder who might have forgotten his key.

"I'm not talking about protecting the house," Fiona O'Brien explained. "I'm worried about you protecting yourself."

No matter how much she needed money for the house upkeep and property taxes, Serena had never risked her own safety or the other tenants' safety by renting to someone unsavory.

"I do background checks on all the boarders," she said. When she'd rented to Stanley, she had also done background checks on Cody, since he was paying most of Stanley's rent. In addition to no criminal record, he had excellent credit. "I'm safe here."

Tammy Ingles picked up a magazine from the old chest in the sitting area at the end of the kitchen. She waved it back and forth in front of her glistening face. Despite the heat, the beautician's makeup was perfect, just like the artful curls in her colorfully streaked hair. "You're not safe anymore."

"I might be in danger of melting," Serena said. The repairman wasn't able to come out for a few days, so she had no relief from the heat. Though it didn't seem quite as hot in the house since Cody had left.

He had been gone for hours. How long had the Hot-shots meeting been? Or had the fire call kept him occupied?

Or a woman?

A pang of jealousy struck her heart. But she drew in a breath and reminded herself his seeing someone else would be for the best. She needed Cody's money more than his fleeting attention.

"You have to stay strong," Fiona said. "Don't let him melt you."

"Him?" she asked. "I was talking about the broken air conditioner."

"Better the AC be broken than your heart," Fiona warned her.

Her heart was breaking, but the lawsuit—not a man—was the cause. However, she hadn't mentioned the lawsuit to her friends. There was nothing they could do to help her. Neither of the women had the kind of money she needed.

"What are you talking about?" she asked Fiona.

"Cody Mallehan," Fiona said. "Wyatt told me he's moved in here."

"Is that why you two stopped in to visit?" She'd been happy to see her friends for a few reasons. She missed them. She was usually so busy with the house and her boarders that she didn't get to see them as much as she liked. She'd also welcomed the distraction from her worries about the house and from her preoccupation with her new boarder.

"You don't get to town much," Tammy said.

She didn't get to town, but the town seemed to come to her—with the gossip her boarders and her friends brought back to her. A smile pulled up the corners of her mouth. "You've mentioned him to me before," she reminded them. "And even if you hadn't, you don't think I could figure out for myself what a womanizer he is?"

Fiona groaned. "He already hit on you."

Tammy snorted. "Of course, he hit on her. He's Cody. He hits on you and Avery all the time—even though you're with his friends."

"He does that just to irritate Wyatt and Dawson," Fiona said.

"He does it because he can't help but flirt with any female with a pulse," Tammy said.

Tammy would understand that behavior; she had a reputation of being quite the flirt herself. Serena suspected this was because of Tammy's awkward teens. Now that she'd lost the weight and cleared up her complexion, their brunette friend enjoyed male attention. But with Tammy it was mostly just flirting. Apparently Cody did more than just flirt.

Serena chuckled. "So you're saying I shouldn't take his attention personally? He's going to hit on Mrs. Gulliver too? She is pretty cute."

Tammy smiled. "Don't you love the pink streaks I put in her hair?"

"She loves them, too," Serena assured the stylist. "She's been talking about adding some purple ones."

Tammy clapped her hands together. "That's great.

She's eighty-six and open to change. When are *you* going to let me change your hair?"

Serena shrugged. "I don't have time."

But she actually kept it long and straight, because it reminded her of how her mother always wore her hair.

"Exactly," Tammy said. "You're too busy to deal with all that hair. Let me cut it off for you."

"Hell no!" a deep voice exclaimed. Cody rushed into the kitchen as if ready to throw himself between Serena and a pair of scissors. "That would be a crime."

Wyatt sauntered in behind his friend. "You're a fire-fighter, not a cop," he reminded Cody. Then he pulled his fiancée into his arms and planted a big kiss on her—as if he hadn't seen her in days, instead of hours.

Serena felt that pang of jealousy again; she was envious of her friend. She wanted that kind of love—that kind of connection.

Cody was here. Staying in the same house. And he apparently liked her hair. But he wasn't looking for love. Even without her friends' warnings, she would have recognized that.

"Cutting hair is not a crime," Tammy said.

"Cutting *her* hair would be," he insisted. And he reached out as if to finger one of the long strands. But he caught himself and pulled his hand back to his side.

Serena's face heated with embarrassment that she and her hair had become the topic of conversation. "What I decide to do about my hair is unimportant," she said. "Have you learned anything more about the arsonist?"

Hopefully they'd caught him. She couldn't get over

how close she had come to losing her home in the last big fire. She gazed around the kitchen at the cabinets she and Mama had stripped and re-stained a rich chocolate color, several shades lighter than the oak floor they'd also refinished. There was no part of the house—structure, contents or residents—that Serena and her mother hadn't cared for.

"Yes," Fiona chimed in, "do you have any leads yet?"

Wyatt sighed and shook his head.

And Cody clenched his jaw so tightly a muscle twitched in his cheek. They were clearly troubled that they hadn't caught the guy yet.

Serena's nurturing instincts—inherited from Mama—kicked in and she turned toward the refrigerator. "I saved you some dinner," she said. "There's enough for everyone." She pulled out the fried chicken and potato salad she'd made earlier.

Fiona groaned. "If I didn't have an appointment to try on wedding gowns, I'd take you up on that offer. But I need to watch what I'm eating."

"No, you don't," Wyatt said as his hand slid over the curve of his fiancée's hip. "You're perfect just as you are."

The envy kicked in again. But she couldn't be jealous of her friend. Fiona deserved her happiness.

Tammy emitted a wistful sigh. "You two make me sick." It was clear she wanted what they had, too.

Cody was the only one who didn't seem envious. His focus was on the chicken instead. He pulled a leg from the bowl she'd set on the counter. But he looked at her as he bit through the crispy coating. Then he moaned with pleasure.

That moan had her stomach muscles clenching in reaction.

"I can heat it up," she offered.

He shook his head. "It's perfect just as it is."

Somehow she didn't think they were talking about the chicken anymore. But before he could clarify, other boarders entered the kitchen. Mr. Stehouwer hobbled into the room with his walker. With a big grin, he greeted all the young people. Stanley bounded in with Annie—both bustling with energy.

She was going to have a time keeping that dog out of the house. But she loved the kitchen being as full of people as it had been when her grandmother had been alive, when she'd had so much family living there.

She wanted to fill it with family again. She had to find a way to hang on to the house.

She wasn't going to find the answer in the wicked glint in Cody's green eyes. Even though the rent he paid for himself and for Stanley would fix the air-conditioning unit, it wasn't enough. She had to find a way to pay off that lawsuit and keep her family legacy.

4

FOR THE PAST HOUR Cody had watched Serena charm and entertain everyone in her home. Everyone but him. Besides feeding him leftovers, she had pretty much ignored him. He wasn't used to women ignoring him unless they had fallen for one of his friends instead. But other women—single women—went out of their way to flirt with him and get his attention. Not that he gave them much.

During his couple of years as a Hotshot, he'd learned that significant others didn't last in this profession. The divorce rate was high among Hotshots because of all the time they spent away from home. So there was no point in his getting involved with anyone. He had to stay single.

Maybe Serena wasn't single. Sure, she wasn't wearing a ring, but that didn't mean she wasn't involved with someone. But hadn't Wyatt said something about her being too busy with the boardinghouse to socialize much? Had he been talking about her friendships or romantic relationships?

Cody was curious about her. More than he should be.

Sure, Dawson had offered Cody his place. But the US Forest Service cabin didn't come with the fried chicken he'd just eaten. Or the creamy potato salad or homemade rolls.

Alone now in one of the second-floor bathrooms, he pulled off his shirt and patted his stomach. He had eaten too much. But he was still hungry. Not for food, but for the woman who'd cooked it.

She was beautiful—even more so when she had been so animated with her other boarders and guests. She'd joked and laughed and she'd even flirted a little bit— with everyone but him. He'd gotten a little irritated then, maybe even jealous.

No. He wasn't the jealous type. That was probably just indigestion from overeating. Although he worked out as strenuously as the other guys on the team, he wasn't as careful about what he ate. That might have to change if he lived with Serena for very long. He reached for the button on his jeans and pulled it free. His jeans were tight—not because of what he'd eaten, but because he couldn't stop thinking about Serena.

About that ice cube sliding down her throat to disappear between her full breasts. About what she would look like wearing nothing at all.

His cock was hard and aching for release. Maybe he should have gone into town to find someone who could relieve some of the tension in his body. But, just like thinking about Serena, that also would have been a mistake.

He pulled aside the lacy curtain and vinyl liner. Then he twisted the faucet to cold. If he wanted to sleep, he'd probably have to take a cold shower, so thoughts of her long curtain of black hair didn't keep him awake.

With the water still running cold, he stepped inside the tub and pulled the curtain closed. But the porcelain was slippery, ridiculously slippery, almost as if... His foot flew across the slick surface and sent him tumbling. His head struck the tile wall. Black spots obscured his vision and something dripped into his eye. It was too thick and sticky to be water.

He was bleeding. He reached up to touch his head, but his limbs were tangled beneath him in the slick tub. As if...*as if it was covered in oil*. He struggled to move, but his vision blurred more until he couldn't see at all. And consciousness slipped away.

SERENA HAD JUST undressed when she heard the crash. The sound came from the second floor.

But she heard no shout. No movement at all. All she heard was water running.

She pulled on a thin robe and then hurried down the stairwell. Mr. Tremont had left that morning with an overnight bag and Stanley had taken Annie for a walk, so there was no one else on the second floor. Except for Cody.

Her pulse quickened, but her footsteps slowed as she approached the door to the bathroom. She hesitated a long moment before lifting her hand to knock. She couldn't just walk in on him in the shower.

After that crash she'd heard, she had to make certain that he was all right, though. It was her responsibility as the landlady.

So she knocked again. Louder.

Still no reply.

"Hello?" she called out. "Are you okay?"

No one answered her. Had he fallen and gotten hurt?

"Cody?" she called his name. But she didn't expect a reply now. She gripped the knob and easily turned it. The door was unlocked. She drew in a deep breath and pushed open the door.

Water sprayed out of the showerhead, flying around the room and across the floor. The rod had been knocked down, the curtain and liner tangled beneath the naked body lying in the tub.

She gasped and hurried forward, but her bare feet slipped on the wet floor. She caught herself on the edge of the tub, so that she didn't fall on top of him. Hand shaking, she turned off the water, which was running cold.

"Cody!"

He didn't move. And blood streaked down his handsome face from a cut on his forehead. Calling upon the nursing training she hadn't quite completed, Serena reached for his wrist and closed her fingers lightly around it. His skin was cold, but his pulse beat steadily beneath her fingers. His chest—so muscular with only a light dusting of golden hair—rose and fell as he breathed. That was good.

He didn't need CPR. Then his pulse increased— pounding faster and harder. She glanced at his face to find his green-eyed gaze focused on her.

"Are you okay?" she asked. "What happened?" This was definitely no trick to get her inside the bathroom while he was naked. He was hurt. He was bleeding and his eyes looked dazed.

He just stared at her as if he couldn't hear. Or couldn't understand.

"I'm going to call 911," she said. He needed a doctor. He obviously had a head injury—a concussion or worse. But when she started to move away, he caught her, his hand wrapping tightly around her wrist.

He hadn't lost his strength, despite being hurt. And the cut and swelling bump on his head didn't detract from his good looks.

He was so handsome it really wasn't fair. His blond hair was slick against his head and nearly as dark as the shadow forming on his strong jaw. And his body...

Her mouth dried, and she struggled to swallow the lump of desire filling her throat. He was masculine perfection—every muscle defined in his arms and in his chest and down the rippling washboard of his abdomen. Her gaze dropped lower to his long cock. As she watched, it began to grow even longer as it swelled and hardened.

But he was the one who murmured, "You're so damn beautiful."

She was surprised that he could see her at all. He'd obviously been knocked out cold when he'd fallen.

"You need medical attention," she said as she tried to tug her wrist free.

But he held on tightly, pulling her down so that she dropped to her knees beside the tub. Then he murmured, "I need *your* attention."

"Cody," she said in protest.

But he moved his other hand into her hair, pulling her head down. And his mouth covered hers. He kissed her with a passion she'd never experienced before.

His lips glided across hers. Then his tongue slipped out, swiping across her bottom lip, tasting her.

She gasped at the delicious sensation. His teeth replaced his tongue as he nipped gently on her bottom lip.

A moan rumbled in her throat. She wanted this—this physical contact. She needed it. It had been so long…

With the house and the lawsuit, she hadn't had any time for dating. But maybe she didn't need to date. Maybe she only needed a physical release. Cody could give her that. But then what would happen when he got bored? She would probably lose him and maybe even Stanley as boarders.

Men like Cody Mallehan always got bored.

Unfortunately they were never boring. His kiss ignited a new excitement in her. Her heart raced. Her skin tingled. She wanted him.

His fingers tangled in her hair as he held her head still for his kiss. And he kept kissing her—moving his lips across hers while teasing her with the tip of his tongue.

Just his kiss had her trembling as desire overwhelmed her. Passion heated her blood, had her breasts swelling, her nipples tightening. She felt the pull from their sensitive tips to her core.

One of his hands moved from her hair. His fingers trailed down the side of her neck and then lower—inside the opening of her robe.

"I've been so jealous," he murmured.

"What?" There was no one in her life for him to envy.

His fingers slid down between her breasts. "I've been so jealous…of that damn ice cube."

She shivered as sensations raced through her.

"The ice cube was colder than my touch," he said, misinterpreting the cause of her shiver.

She was beyond hot for him. But his fingers were cold. And she remembered that he'd been lying under the almost icy spray of water. She reached out and touched the bump on his head. The blood was no longer flowing, but it continued to trickle from the cut.

"You might need stitches," she said, "and a CT scan." She'd taken enough nursing courses to know the consequences of a serious concussion. He could develop a bleed and swelling on the brain.

"I need you." He moved in the tub, as if trying to get out, but he slipped again. "What the hell…"

"Don't," she said. "You shouldn't try to move. You might have broken a bone."

"It's not broken," he said.

She glanced down at his erection. And a wistful gasp escaped from her lips. He was so big. So hard…

She wanted to touch him. "You're hurt," she reminded them both.

He groaned. "I'm hurting…"

"Let me call for help—"

But he had her wrist again. When he tugged on it, though, he slipped and inadvertently jerked Serena into the bathtub with him. She tumbled down on top of his naked body. Her silky robe and her skin slid over his.

Her pulse raced. She gripped his arms, trying to steady herself to get up, but instead of pushing away, she held on to him. "Cody…"

He groaned again and touched his fingers to the bump on his head. He was hurting. Really hurting.

And she was thinking only of how amazing his body felt against hers. His cock pushed against her hip, pulsing like her heartbeat. She wanted to touch it, taste it…

But she couldn't act on her desire—for so many reasons. She reached for the tub instead of him, trying to use the porcelain for leverage. But her hand slipped. The surface wasn't just slick from the water. There was something on it—something oily.

She understood now why Cody had fallen. He could have been killed.

5

His body ached with desire. Cody had never wanted anyone more than he wanted Serena Beaumont. His head ached, too. Actually it pounded. He grimaced at the pain and tried to pry open his eyes. The light was so bright, though, that he groaned. Then a dark shadow, leaning over him, mercifully blocked the light.

"Serena," he murmured.

The shadow chuckled—a deep, masculine-sounding chuckle. It definitely wasn't Serena leaning over his naked body.

Cody shifted against the bathroom floor. His butt slid over the wet porcelain tiles, producing a squeaking noise.

The chuckle turned into a loud, echoing laugh. "Jeez, Cody…"

He recognized that voice, and heat rushed to his face.

"Owen, what the hell are you doing here?" he asked. The last thing he remembered was stepping into the shower. How had he wound up on the floor? The only images that flashed through his mind were of Serena, in a thin robe.

Her nipples had pushed against the silky fabric, and then the robe had parted, revealing honey-toned curves...

Was that just a dream, like all the others he'd had about her since they'd first met months ago? But her skin and lips had felt so real.

It was almost as if he could taste her still, the sweetness of her mouth.

A light flashed in his eyes—just a small beam, but it felt like it was shining through his pupil and piercing his brain. "Damn it! Damn it!" He batted at the flashlight. "Shut it off!"

"I am trying to check you out," Owen said.

Since Cody was sprawled naked across the bathroom floor, it shouldn't have been too difficult. At least he wasn't hard anymore—not now that he'd realized it was Owen leaning over him and not Serena.

Where was Serena? He peered around the white-and-blue bathroom, but he and Owen were alone. Had she ever been in there?

"Who called you?"

Had Stanley found him? That poor kid.

"Your landlady," Owen said. "You kept murmuring her name."

"Serena found me?" he asked. So he hadn't imagined it. She had been there while he was naked. "And she called *you*?" She knew Wyatt because she was friends with Fiona. But Owen?

"She called 911," Owen replied. "Remember, I'm a paramedic, too?"

"Yeah, yeah, I know that," Cody said. Fortunately

Dawson wasn't working with him tonight; the assistant superintendent was too busy helping Zimmer try to catch the arsonist to go out on medical calls.

Hell, maybe Dawson *was* in the room too, for all Cody knew. His eyesight was fuzzy, making it hard for him to focus visually and mentally. Owen was still leaning over him with that damn light. The guy was so big—broad-shouldered and tall—he could have been blocking Dawson from Cody's blurry vision.

"What the hell happened?" he asked.

"Don't you remember?" Owen asked, and there was concern in his deep voice and blue eyes. He was older than Cody—not just in years but experience. Cody couldn't imagine what Owen had seen overseas, but the guy had come back with scars—one was visible, running down the left side of his face. He suspected there were more.

Cody shook his head and flinched as pain reverberated throughout his skull. His head was pounding so badly that he was surprised he could remember anything—even his own name. Well, the name the young couple had given him after they'd adopted Baby John Doe.

The last thing he remembered was turning on the water to cold because of *her*.

"You must have slipped and fallen," Owen surmised.

He fought through the pain to make a cocky reply. "You think?"

"You don't remember."

"No." But then he recalled the porcelain had been so slippery. Why?

"Where are your clothes?" Owen asked.

"Clothes?" he repeated. He was still struggling to focus. Where had he left them?

"Some of the nurses have probably already seen you naked, but you should still get dressed before I take you in," Owen said.

"In where?"

"To the hospital," his friend patiently replied.

He was once again glad Serena hadn't called Wyatt or Dawson. He doubted either of them would have been nearly as patient with Cody's befuddled mind.

"Why would I go to the hospital?" he asked as he tried to remember how he'd wound up on the bathroom floor. Had he fallen out of the tub?

Serena wouldn't have been strong enough to move him. It must have been Owen; the guy was huge. How long had Cody been unconscious?

"You need to have a CT," Owen said. "I think you have a concussion."

That would explain the headache and memory lapse. But what about his fantasies about Serena? He'd had those long before he'd ever hit his head. What was wrong with him that he couldn't get the black-haired woman off his mind?

SERENA STARED OUT the attic window into the darkness. Still no lights appeared in the driveway. Should she have gone to the hospital with him? Cody's coworker had taken him in hours ago. Seeing Owen James again—in this house—had been hard because it had reminded her of the day she'd lost her mother.

That horrible day when she had felt so helpless…

But, this time, Owen had assured her that Cody wasn't seriously injured. He only wanted to get him checked out at the hospital—get him the CT she'd suspected he needed and stitches for the laceration on his forehead.

Should she have ridden along with him anyway? Or followed the ambulance as Stanley had?

Was he truly all right?

Head injuries could be dangerous. Not only had he lost consciousness, he'd nearly lost control with her.

What was her excuse?

She hadn't hit her head. Why had she kissed him back? Why had she wanted him, a self-professed player?

Unable to bear the silence and all the thoughts flitting through her mind any longer, she picked up her cell phone and hit Fiona's number. It was late, but her friend answered right away.

"Serena?" She must have looked at her caller ID.

"Do you know that Cody got hurt tonight?"

"Yes, Wyatt, Dawson and Braden went up to meet him and Owen at the hospital," she replied.

It must have been bad for Wyatt and his fellow Hotshots to go to the hospital, too. Owen hadn't let Cody walk out of the house; he'd had Stanley help carry him out on a stretcher.

She should have gone, too. It would have been better than pacing her apartment.

"Has Wyatt called to let you know how he is?" she anxiously asked.

"Yeah, Wyatt told me he's on his way home." That

must have been why Fiona was awake; she was waiting for her fiancé.

"What did he say about Cody?"

"He's fine," Fiona assured her. "He has a slight concussion. But his pride is what's hurting most." The other
woman chuckled. "Probably because he knows the guys
will never let him live it down."

"Live what down?" she asked. "It was an accident.
He slipped."

"Exactly," Fiona said. "Hotshots have these extraor-
dinarily dangerous jobs, but he got hurt taking a shower.
They're going to razz him about it."

"He fell because the tub was unusually slippery,"
Serena said. Why? She had washed it earlier that day
after he'd left for his meeting, and she didn't think anyone had used it after that. "Do you think he'll sue me?"

"Sue you? Why?" Fiona asked. As Serena's insurance agent, she should have been concerned.

"Because he was hurt in my house." Maybe the
cleaner she'd used on the tub had made it oily. Could she
have caused his fall? A pang of regret struck her heart;
she hoped she wasn't responsible for him getting hurt.

"I doubt it," Fiona assured her. "From what I know
about Cody, he doesn't seem to care about money or
possessions or anything but having a good time—
whether he's with a woman or fighting a fire."

"But how well do you really know him?" Serena
asked. As far as she was aware, she was the only one
who knew that he paid half of Stanley's room and board.
How did he have enough money to be that generous?

"I know he's an incorrigible flirt," Fiona said. "He's cocky and funny and competitive."

"And?" she prodded. She wanted to know more about Cody than his clean criminal background and good credit could tell her. On her circuit of pacing, she passed her bed. She loved the old brass frame—loved that so many of her ancestors had slept on it. Her grandmother had even been born on that bed. But Serena couldn't look at it now without imagining Cody in it, naked and sexy.

"Are you curious about Cody just because you're worried he's going to sue you?" Fiona asked. "Or are you interested in him?"

Serena snorted; she didn't care how unladylike it was. "He's not my type." She had never gone for the sexy, cocky guy. Of course she had never stumbled across a naked one before either.

"No, he's not," Fiona wholeheartedly agreed. "You want a guy who will settle down and raise a family here in Northern Lakes."

Her friend might not have known Cody all that well, but she knew Serena. Of course she had never made any secret of how much she loved her hometown and, most especially, her house.

"And Cody's not that guy," Fiona continued. "He can't wait to leave Northern Lakes again."

"But he comes back…" Unlike Serena's twin, who had left Northern Lakes after high school and never returned—not even for their mother's funeral. Courtney had never made any secret of how much she'd hated her hometown.

And apparently her home…

"You do like him!" Fiona accused her. Before Serena could deny it again, her friend added, "I get it. Wyatt isn't my type either."

"Then why are you marrying him?" If she was considering changing her mind, Serena and Tammy might want to hold off on the bachelorette party. They weren't getting too far with the planning anyway. Serena wanted to have it at the house while Tammy wanted to go to some new club on male stripper night.

"Because I love him," Fiona answered, as if it was just that simple.

But Serena knew better. Her mother had loved her father. But he hadn't reciprocated, or he wouldn't have left her. While she wished her friend luck, Serena wasn't going to fall for someone who didn't want the same things out of life that she did.

It would only end painfully. Her mother had never recovered from that broken heart either. She'd never married. She'd barely even dated. Her only loves had been her daughters, her family and her home.

"I just want to know if Cody will sue me," Serena said. She already had one lawsuit she couldn't afford to pay; she couldn't deal with another.

Fiona sighed. "I can't tell you if he'll sue. People file lawsuits for the most bizarre reasons."

Serena knew that all too well. She hadn't expected the lawsuit at all, and she suspected she didn't know the real reason for it. She sighed, too. "Then it's very possible that he could."

"He could," Fiona admitted. "But he's Cody. And you're pretty."

She was no beauty like her mother, but, thanks to her genes, she *was* pretty. "What does what I look like have to do with anything?"

"I think you could easily dissuade him from suing you."

Lights glinted off the glass of the dormer window as a vehicle headed toward the house. Someone was coming home. Just Stanley or was Cody with him? If he was, she might know soon enough whether or not he was litigious.

"How?" she asked.

"I'll give you the same advice Tammy gave me when I wanted Wyatt's help to dissuade Matthew from quitting college to become a firefighter." Matt was Fiona's younger brother, and she was very protective of him. In Matt's opinion, she was overprotective. He hadn't been hired, though, and had voluntarily decided to return to college and get his degree—just like his big sister had hoped.

Serena could already imagine what Tammy's advice had been, but she found herself asking anyway. "And what was that?"

"Seduce him."

"Fiona!" she exclaimed. It was an outrageous idea. Her friend laughed. She knew it was.

"Is that the advice of my insurance agent?" Serena asked. "Or my friend?"

"I'm kidding," Fiona said. "I know you would never do that."

But Serena flashed back to finding a naked Cody knocked out in the bathtub. Remembering how he'd touched her, how he'd kissed her, her skin heated. Maybe it wasn't that outrageous of an idea.

6

A KNOCK RATTLED the bedroom door, echoing the pounding in Cody's head. Maybe he should have filled the prescription for painkillers the ER doctor had given him. But Cody hated taking pills. Growing up he'd had more than enough from the foster parents, counselors and social workers who'd tried putting him on every kind of ADHD medication—no matter that he had never been diagnosed. He'd just been an active kid, and they'd wanted to calm him down to comatose.

No, he'd had enough pills to last him a lifetime. He could handle the pain. If the pounding stopped...

"It's open," he called out before his visitor knocked again.

The old hinges creaked as the heavy mahogany door opened. He expected it to be Stanley, checking on him again as he had throughout the night. Had the doctor scared the kid with talk about bleeding on the brain and loss of consciousness? Or had Stanley felt guilty? Had he done something to make the bathtub as slippery as it had been?

While Stanley had been driving him home last night,

Cody had asked him, "So what was that? Some kind of hazing?"

Growing up they'd been through it all every time they'd gone to a new foster home. Cody couldn't imagine it had been any better for Stanley than it had been for him. Stanley had been befuddled, though. "What was what?"

"Sliming my tub so I'd fall—you did that, right?" Cody had asked.

And Stanley had been so hurt that he'd looked like Cody had struck him. Hard. He was too upset to be faking, and he'd kept checking to make sure Cody was okay. He was a good kid.

Cody had realized that when they'd met a little over nine years ago. Stanley had been slow but sweet. So Cody had defended him from kids who would have picked on him. He'd kept in touch with Stanley throughout the years and brought him to Northern Lakes when Stanley had had to leave the foster home in Detroit.

Now, Stanley loved living in Northern Lakes and had been so grateful to Cody for bringing him there.

"I'm sorry about before," Cody said as the door opened farther. "It was just the concussion talking."

"What do you mean?" It wasn't Stanley who asked the question. The voice—though husky—was feminine. And so was the curvy body that stepped into the room, clad again in cutoff shorts and a tank top.

"I thought you were Stanley," he said, and he shifted against the mattress so he could get a better look at Serena.

She glanced down at herself. "I haven't been mistaken for a teenage boy in a while."

"Probably never," Cody said with an appreciative sigh.

"Maybe when I was twelve," she said. "Did you hit on Stanley last night, too?"

So he hadn't dreamed that scene in the steamy bathroom. He had touched her. He had kissed her. "No, apparently just you," he said.

She stepped closer to the bed—but not close enough for him to reach for her, to pull her down into the bed with him. He wanted to feel her—to kiss her—now that his mind was clear and he could remember every detail and sensation.

"Don't I deserve an apology, then?" she asked.

He shrugged. "What would be the point when I intend to do it again?"

He hadn't intended to do it at all. He didn't need to complicate his life by hitting on his landlady. But now that he'd crossed that line, he couldn't uncross it. He couldn't pretend—to himself or her—that he didn't want her.

Even if he tried to lie now, his body would betray him. His erection tented the thin sheet he'd pulled over himself. Maybe that was why she stayed out of reach. But she must not have realized how long his arms were. He moved quickly, pulling her down onto the bed beside him before she was able to escape.

But she didn't fight him. Instead she flopped down on her back, laughed and murmured, "You do like living dangerously."

"That's the truth." He put himself in danger all the time—fighting fires, driving too fast, hitting on other guys' women. He hadn't thought taking a shower would prove to be the most hazardous thing he'd done lately.

But what about her? Would she cause him pain?

She looked so damn beautiful lying beside him, her hair strewn across his pillow—just as he'd imagined so many times over the past few months. He propped himself up on an elbow and leaned over her. She stared up at him, her eyes so wide and dark.

"Are you going to hurt me?" he asked.

Her voice a husky whisper, she said, "I was just going to ask you the same thing."

He hadn't thought he'd scared her. "I would never hurt a woman," he assured her.

"Maybe not physically," she agreed. "What about emotionally?"

Maybe he shouldn't have worked so hard to make people think he was a player. But that protected them as much as it protected him. "Your friends Fiona and Tammy warned you about me?"

She nodded. "Should I believe everything I hear?"

The way she was staring up at him—as if she could see right through him—was unnerving. Nobody had ever looked at him like that, like they actually saw the real him. But then she knew about how he was helping Stanley.

Realizing that he was still clasping her wrist, he ran his fingers up her bare arm to her shoulder. Then he leaned down farther so his lips nearly brushed hers as he replied, "You better believe it."

"So you are a heartbreaker," she said with an almost regretful sigh.

He shook his head. "No," he assured her with all seriousness. "Someone actually has to love you for you to be able to break their heart."

"Nobody's ever loved you?" she asked. And now there was something in her dark eyes he hated seeing more than anything else: pity.

The poor orphan. The kid nobody wanted to keep...

He forced a laugh, like he always had. "Only because I don't give anyone the chance," he said. "I take off before things can get serious."

She drew in a deep breath—which pushed her breasts against the thin material of her lacy bra and her tank top. "I didn't need any warning," she said.

"You already had my number?"

She shook her head. "You do a better job pushing people away from you than anyone else could." The pity was gone from her gaze now, but she was still looking at him in the way that told him she really saw him. And maybe even understood him.

Now he was the one who was afraid. Nobody had ever gotten to know him so well—so quickly.

"What did you do to Stanley if you didn't hit on him, too?" she asked.

In a ragged sigh, he released the breath he hadn't realized he'd been holding until his chest had begun to hurt. Regret filled him—regret for what he'd said to Stanley and for pulling Serena into bed with him. "I accused him of pranking me."

"Pranking you?" she asked, her brow furrowing.

"By rubbing oil on the tub, so I would slip and fall."

"Stanley would never do anything to hurt you," she said. "He worships you."

He didn't know about the worship part, but he knew the kid wouldn't hurt a fly, much less a person. Too bad people hadn't always treated him with the same care. Too bad Cody hadn't last night. "I know *he* didn't do it."

"But you think someone else did?"

He nodded. The tub hadn't just been oily like someone had taken a bubble bath; it had been slicked down with something like petroleum jelly—so there was no way he could have avoided falling.

Although it didn't quite reach her eyes, her lips curved into a teasing smile. "Couldn't you just be clumsy?"

"I'm not," he said. And he suspected she knew it. He wouldn't have survived his job—wielding chain saws and other heavy equipment—if he was. He would have lost a limb or his head before now. "Someone had to have sabotaged the tub."

"It was slippery," she admitted. "But who would purposely do something so juvenile?"

"I don't know," he admitted. Even if the older residents had reverted to their second childhoods, they wouldn't have been able to climb the stairs. And he hadn't even seen the other tenant yet. That left only her and Stanley.

"None of your ex-girlfriends live here," she teased.

He continued to stare down at her; she was so beautiful—so tempting—lying next to him. Why hadn't she moved? "Not yet."

Her dark eyes narrowed. He couldn't tell if she was playing or really offended when she asked, "Are you implying that I'll be your next ex?"

He moved closer, so that his erection nudged her hip. "I want you."

Did she want him? She hadn't jumped up from his bed. And he hadn't imagined her in the bathroom with him the night before. Had she kissed him back?

He had to know. He had to kiss her again. He lowered his head and tentatively moved his mouth across hers. Her breath—so sweet and warm—sighed across his lips. He deepened the kiss, parted her lips and dipped his tongue inside.

She gasped. But she didn't pull away. She kissed him back—just as he'd imagined. Her tongue flitted across his, teasing him.

He groaned. He'd already been hard just thinking about her. But now he ached. He rolled her against him so they lay front to front. Her breasts pushed against his bare chest. He could feel the hardness of her nipples. He moved one hand beneath her tank top and found the clasp of her bra lying against the curve of her spine. A flick of his finger undid it.

She gasped and pulled her mouth from his. "You are too good at that."

He'd just gotten lucky. But he tensed, worrying that his luck was about to run out. She was looking at him, but not like she had before; now she was seeing the player she'd heard about.

But that was better—for both of them. She wouldn't

expect too much from him, then. She wouldn't get too close emotionally.

Physically she wasn't close enough. But the space she had put between them allowed him to pull up her tank top, so that he could see the breasts he'd freed. He pushed up the shirt and the white lace bra. Desire overwhelmed him. Her breasts were perfectly round and full, the nipples puckered and waiting for his touch. He brushed a fingertip across one.

A moan escaped her. She was so responsive, her body instinctively arching toward him.

He lowered his mouth and closed his lips around that point. He tugged on it gently.

She lifted her hands to his hair, running her fingers through it before her fingers touched the bandage covering the stitches on his head. Then she tensed.

"You're hurt," she said, as if she'd just remembered.

At the moment, he didn't give a damn. "I'm fine."

"You have a concussion," she reminded him—or maybe it was herself she was reminding. "We can't do this…"

He pushed his straining cock against her hip. "I can."

He needed to do this, to bury himself inside her.

"No," she said. "This is a bad idea. You're not thinking clearly."

"What about you?" he asked.

"I'm not thinking clearly either," she said. "I came in here to check on you, not—"

"—sleep with me?" he teased.

Her face, already a pretty tan, flushed red with embarrassment.

"Or did you?"

And finally she moved. She tugged her shirt down and rolled out of bed, dropping to her knees next to it. "Of course not. I wouldn't. Fiona wasn't even serious—"

Before she could scramble any farther away from him, he caught her wrist. "About what?"

"Me seducing you…"

He gasped in shock. "What?"

And she shook her head. "No, no, she wasn't serious. She just said that so you wouldn't sue me. She's my insurance agent and you got hurt on my property. So she told me to…"

"Seduce me." Now he managed to laugh. That was the last thing he would have suspected anyone—let alone a friend of hers—to suggest.

"She was kidding," Serena said. "She told me that you wouldn't sue anyway."

"Hmm…" He acted like he was considering it. But he must have been a better actor than he'd thought because now her skin grew pale and she began to tremble. "Of course I wouldn't," he assured her. "I'm fine."

"That's good," she said. "That's why I came in here—to see if you needed anything."

"Just you."

She shook her head. "No. You're my boarder. We can't get involved."

"It would be a bad idea," he reluctantly agreed.

She nodded.

"You would fall all crazy in love with me," he teased. "And then I'd break your heart when I leave."

Her face was still pale, but she emitted a faint laugh. "Yeah, right…"

"I will leave," he told her. He'd put in his two seasons with the Hotshots to get the experience needed for smoke jumping. Once a position opened, it was his. It had to be—because he had to leave. Soon. Maybe even sooner if she kept looking at him that way.

Like she knew him. He had to make sure she really did. "I always leave," he warned.

"Why?" she asked.

"Because it's better that way."

"Better for whom?"

Better for him, but he'd learned that the hard way. When he'd been younger, he had naively gotten attached, first to those adoptive parents—or so his social worker had told him—and then to other foster families. He'd started thinking he was staying only to be moved to another home. Now he was older and wiser. He knew to move along before he got attached to anyone. Then he couldn't get rejected.

"It's better for everyone," he assured her. "I don't get bored, and nobody gets hurt." He wasn't just protecting himself this time. He was protecting her.

So MUCH FOR seducing him into not suing her. He'd found the very idea hilarious—as if she couldn't have succeeded. Not that she would have tried. So Serena's pride shouldn't have been stung when he'd laughed.

Or when he'd agreed that it would be a bad idea for them to sleep together. It wasn't as if she had time for a relationship anyway.

At least she only had one lawsuit to worry about; Cody obviously had no intention of suing her. He probably wouldn't stick around long enough to file a suit. Hopefully he would pay his and Stanley's room and board for a few more months, though.

She needed proof of that income in order to apply for a mortgage or a business loan. She had no idea what else she needed to qualify. But she intended to find out.

She fished out a card from the bottom of her purse. It was bent and worn from knocking around with her wallet and hand lotion and coupon container. She had to tilt it toward the light streaming through the crescent-shaped window above her brass headboard in order to read the phone number and punch the digits into her cell.

"Gordon Townsend," a pleasant-sounding voice greeted her. Fortunately the number he'd given her was his direct line.

"Hi, Gordon, this is Serena Beaumont."

"Serena!" he exclaimed, his delight obvious. "I've been hoping you would call me."

"You have?" If the bank was that anxious to hand out money, maybe she would actually have a shot at getting a mortgage on the home or a business loan for the boardinghouse.

"Of course I have. I gave you my card a while ago," he said. "So I had kind of given up hope of hearing from you."

Gordon had given her his card when they'd run into each other at the grocery store. Since it had been his professional card, she thought he'd just been drumming up business for the bank. She hadn't realized his interest could be personal.

"I'm sorry," she murmured.

"It's fine," he said. "You've called now. That's the important thing. I thought you might already be involved with someone."

She nearly laughed. Her only relationship since her mom had died had been with the house and her boarders. But if she'd had time to date, she might have considered Gordon; he was her type. He was a hometown guy who had come back after college because he'd missed Northern Lakes. He wanted to settle down and raise a family in the safe, friendly small town where he had grown up. He also had a good job. He was well-known and respected.

No one would warn her to stay away from Gordon. He wouldn't hurt her or abandon her. But he probably wouldn't excite her either—not like Cody had. Even now—hours after lying in bed with him—her pulse pounded and her skin tingled. And she would never get the image out of her mind of his naked body: his sculpted muscles, his engorged…

"No!" she said—to stop herself from thinking about sleeping with Cody. That wouldn't have been just a bad idea but a disastrous one.

"So, you're not in a relationship?"

"No, no," Serena stammered, "I'm too busy trying to get my business established."

"Yes, I've heard you started a boardinghouse," he said.

"Mom already had it going." She'd had Mrs. Gulliver

and Mr. Stehouwer living with her. When Serena had dropped out of nursing school, she'd come home to help her mom care for the octogenarians.

Unfortunately she hadn't been able to help her mother, though, when she'd found her on the landing of the back stairwell. The heart attack had killed her instantly.

She blinked away the tears stinging her eyes and focused on the conversation. "I have more boarders now." Thanks to Cody. "So I'm calling to make an appointment to discuss some financing with you."

"Oh, oh," Gordon said with apparent disappointment. "I'm sorry I misunderstood."

"I'm sorry too," she said—sorry that she'd been so oblivious when he'd given her his card. She'd been so focused on her grocery list and coupons that she hadn't talked to him very long. They'd just exchanged a few quick pleasantries and he'd given her his card.

"So dating's not out of the question?" Gordon asked hopefully.

He was her type—she reminded herself.

"No," she said. "It's not…"

But she made a bank appointment, not a date, for the following week. She told herself that it was just because she didn't want to date anyone right now.

Not because she was interested in Cody.

7

"NEVER FIGURED YOU for the bubble bath kind," Ethan Sommerly needled him, his lips curving into a wide grin within his bushy black beard.

How the hell did he stand all that hair on his face in this heat? But maybe it only felt hot to Cody because he kept thinking about Serena, in his bed, about kissing her...

"What?" Cody asked.

Superintendent Zimmer had just wrapped up another Hotshots meeting at the firehouse. All twenty members of the team had been present in the third-floor conference room. They milled around now, drinking coffee and snacking on cookies and brownies.

The brownies were probably the best thing about the meeting. They had no news about the arsonist and no leads. Fortunately the arsonist hadn't set any more fires, though. So Braden had said that the next time they were called up to help out with the fires out west, they would go to relieve the crews currently working them.

Cody waited, but he didn't feel that usual surge of excitement at the idea of traveling again, of exploring a new place and conquering another blaze. Maybe he'd hit his head harder than he'd thought.

Usually he enjoyed these meetings. He loved getting together with the entire team and laughing and joking. But while everyone else had migrated toward those snack tables at the back, he had moved to the windows with a view of the village of Northern Lakes. It was a cute little tourist town with quaint-looking shops and restaurants.

"Owen said you took a tumble in the tub," Ethan said, gesturing at Cody's head. "Guess those bubble baths can be dangerous."

The bandage was gone, but he had another couple of days before the stitches would be removed.

"I was taking a shower," he said, "not a bath."

"Never figured you were so clumsy," Trent Miles chimed in as he walked up behind them. He wasn't as big and burly as Sommerly, but the guy was every bit as tough. The fires he fought during the off-season were even more dangerous than the wildfires—because he fought them in the most violent area of Detroit. Cody had always thought he was fearless until he said, "You got me scared, Mallehan."

Cody snorted. "How's that?"

"Not sure I want to be running a saw with you," Miles replied. "What if you slip again?"

He knew these guys wouldn't believe that someone else had caused his fall. Unless he gave them a reason...

"I won't be *distracted* on the line," he assured his team members, assuming his usual arrogant attitude.

"You were distracted in the shower?" Ethan asked, arching a bushy brow.

Yes, with thoughts of his hot landlady. Or he might have noticed that the tub had been tampered with before he'd stepped into it.

Trent groaned. "I think that's Mallehan subtle way of letting us know he hadn't been alone."

He had been but not for long. Serena had rushed to his rescue. But she would have done that for anyone. It was her nature to care for others. Over the past few days that he'd been sidelined with the concussion, he'd watched her take care of the other boarders.

She treated Mrs. Gulliver, with her pink-streaked hair, more like a grandmother than a boarder. She brought her tea and cookies to munch on while the old woman watched her soap operas. She flirted with dirty old Mr. Stehouwer more than she'd ever flirted with Cody. She treated Stanley like a kid brother. And over the past few days, she'd treated Cody like an invalid, making sure he had aspirin and rest.

Hell, despite her not wanting the mutt in her house, she took care of Annie, too. The overgrown puppy adored her, just like everyone else. She followed Serena from room to room. Cody had wanted to follow her, too.

It was good he'd had the meeting to attend—a reason to escape the house and his feelings for her. His desire.

He wanted her. That was all it was: attraction. Nothing else.

That was why he couldn't get her out of his mind. Even now he thought he saw her on the street below.

Was there another woman in town who had black hair that long and silky-looking?

She had just stepped out of the bank down the street. Her slender shoulders were slumped, and she lifted her hand to her face, as if brushing something from her cheek. Tears?

What had upset her?

Someone snapped fingers in his face, drawing his attention away from the window. He turned around expecting to see Trent and Ethan. But it was Braden who stood in front of him.

"You okay?" his boss asked.

He gazed around the room and realized everyone else had left. "Sure. Yeah, of course I am."

"You seem out of it," Zimmer said.

He'd been distracted. He glanced back to the window, but the black-haired woman was gone. Had it been Serena? Or was he only imagining her everywhere?

"I'm not sure you should have come back yet," his boss said.

"The doctor cleared me," he reminded Braden. He'd had to get a note to prove that he was physically ready for the demands of his job. Of course it hadn't been all that demanding lately. Maybe that was why he'd been so edgy; he was just restless. It had nothing to do with Serena at all.

Braden nodded. "Yeah, you've got the medical clearance." His brown eyes narrowed as he studied Cody's face. His look was uncomfortably close to how Serena looked at him. But it was clear Braden was still trying to understand him. It was like Serena already did. "What about the *mental* clearance?"

"What do you mean?" But he was afraid that he knew. And it wasn't just restlessness. He'd been restless before, but he'd never felt like this.

"You okay?" Zimmer asked again. "You seem really preoccupied."

Damn Serena.

"Just antsy to get back to work," he said. And away from the temptation that was Serena Beaumont.

"This season has been hard on you," Braden acknowledged.

Cody shook his head. "It's been easier than any other one. We've spent most of it here in Northern Lakes." Waiting for the damn arsonist to strike again.

"That's why it's been hard," Braden said. "You've been stuck in one place. I know that's not easy on you."

It wasn't easy because it wasn't familiar.

"I get it," Cody said. "It's our responsibility to protect Northern Lakes."

"It's mine," Braden said. Maybe it was because he was the boss—maybe it was just his personality—but he always assumed responsibility for everything.

Cody had no doubt that Braden would stop the arsonist if it was the last thing he did.

"But we're a team," Cody reminded him. "You don't have to do it alone."

"I know that," Braden said. With a pointed stare, he added, "*I'm* not the loner."

Cody was; he'd made no secret of that. But that didn't mean he didn't care about the team.

"Have I done something you're upset about?" he asked as his heart began to beat harder, like it had every time his social worker had showed up and he'd just known he was moving again. "The concussion wasn't my fault."

He wasn't sure whose fault it was, though. Maybe it had just been an accident. But he had a niggling feeling that wasn't the case.

Braden shook his head and sighed. "No, you didn't do anything. You made your position clear when I hired you. You only wanted to do a couple of seasons as a Hotshot before becoming a smoke jumper."

That had been his plan; it seemed like so long ago now. "True."

"Mack McRooney recommended I hire you," Braden said.

Two years ago Cody, who'd already been working as a firefighter with the US Forest Service, had trained to be a smoke jumper with a dozen other guys. McRooney had put them through rigorous physical training—which had weeded them down to just Cody and a couple of other guys. Cody had worked hard; he had gotten good at parachuting out of planes. But there had only been one position open at that time, and Mack had given it to a guy with Hotshot experience.

Cody nodded. "He told me about the position on your team." The job had sent him back to Michigan from Washington. Michigan was where he'd grown up after being dropped at a fire station in Detroit.

"He called me the other day to check on you," Braden said.

"How'd he know about my accident? And why would he care?" Cody wondered aloud. He'd liked the older guy, but they hadn't kept in touch.

"He wants to know if you're ready to make the switch," Braden replied, "if you have enough practical experience to become a smoke jumper."

Cody had wanted that job for so long that he expected another surge of excitement. But he felt only mild curiosity. "He has an open position?"

Braden nodded. Then his brow furrowed with confusion. "You must not be completely recovered yet."

"Why do you say that?"

"I thought you'd jump at the chance to apply for that jumper position."

"Ha-ha," he said in response to his boss's bad pun. "Of course I'll apply." He'd already stayed too long with the Huron Hotshots. He was in danger of getting attached not just to his team members, but to a certain black-haired beauty as well.

"THANKS FOR MEETING ME here," Serena said when her friends slid into the booth across from her.

Until they arrived, she'd felt out of place in the working-class bar. Not only had she been one of the only females, she'd also felt overdressed in the skirt and blouse she'd worn for her bank appointment. She was lucky she hadn't tripped as she'd crossed the peanut-strewn wood floor in her heels.

Fiona and Tammy had easily maneuvered across the room in their heels. But then they were more used to dressing up than Serena was.

"We're thrilled you finally got out of that house," Tammy said.

Serena blinked, fighting off the tears that threatened. These weren't tears of sadness like when she thought of her mother. These were tears of frustration.

"What's wrong?" Fiona asked, reaching across the table for Serena's hands. The diamond on the redhead's finger caught and refracted the light that swung over the booth.

"What did Cody do?" Tammy asked, her brown eyes narrowing with immediate suspicion.

"Is he suing you?" Fiona asked.

Serena shook her head. "Cody didn't do anything." Which could be part of the reason for her frustration. After that afternoon when they'd realized what a bad idea sleeping together would be, he hadn't hit on her again. The other part of her frustration she didn't want to think, let alone talk, about…

"If it's not Cody, then what's wrong?" Fiona persisted.

Serena blinked again and forced a bright smile. "Why does something have to be wrong for me to call my friends for drinks?"

"Oh, something's definitely up," Tammy said. She raised her hand and waved over a waitress. "And we'll get it out of you once we get you liquored up."

Serena laughed, a real laugh that eased the tight pressure in her chest. This was why she'd called her friends—to get her mind off her troubles and off Cody. If she'd gone home and run into him again…

She wasn't sure what she might have done. She might

have dragged him to her bed. If she let Tammy liquor her up, she still might.

"You are not getting me drunk," she insisted with another laugh. She couldn't remember the last time she'd been out with them, though, and it felt good. So she didn't protest when Tammy ordered a round of shots.

She picked up and downed her Fireball, then sputtered, "I hope you know one of you is driving me home."

"Oh, we'll get you a ride," Tammy promised. She drank her own shot. Then she called for another round. She obviously didn't intend to be the designated driver. Of course she lived in town and could walk home from the Filling Station.

Fiona slapped her empty shot glass back on the table. "Good thing Wyatt's meeting me here when he's done at the firehouse," she said, "because I'm not sure I'll be able to walk home if we keep drinking like this."

"Is he bringing any hunky Hotshot friends with him?" Tammy asked with a salacious smile.

"Dawson," Fiona said, "but you had your chance. He's taken now."

"Dawson and I were just friends," Tammy said.

They'd told her how he had saved her from the bar fight. For some reason Serena was glad that it hadn't been Cody.

Tammy arched a perfect brow and asked, "What about their super-sexy boss? Is he coming, too?"

"Braden?" Fiona turned back toward Serena. "I don't know why I didn't think of it before."

Serena wasn't certain she liked the way her friend was staring at her. "What?"

"You and Braden," Fiona said. She snapped her fingers. "He's so your type."

"Why isn't he *my* type?" Tammy asked with a pout. She considered every man her type.

"He's too nice for you," Fiona said with the bluntness with which only longtime friends could speak to each other.

"Hey!" Tammy said. But the twinkle in her eyes suggested she was only acting offended.

"You'd break his heart," Fiona said. "And he's just getting over a bad relationship."

"And that makes him my type?" Serena asked. She'd never had her heart broken—except when her mother had died. She'd never loved anyone else enough to miss them like she still missed her mother.

She'd had boyfriends in high school, in college. But they hadn't been serious ones—no one she had envisioned raising her family with in her ancestral home. She hadn't been ready for that then anyway. And now she might never have the chance…

"He's a really great guy," Fiona said. "He's responsible and dependable—the kind of man you can count on."

Serena smiled. Her friend did know her well.

Fiona turned toward Tammy. "You and Cody should really get together. You're both flirts."

"No!" Serena said.

"What?" Tammy asked. "Are you staking a claim on him?"

Serena shook her head. "Nobody will ever be able to

claim Cody Mallehan," she said. He'd made that clear to her.

But that was good. She didn't have time for romance right now.

Tammy touched Serena's empty shot glass. "This *is* about him."

"Not at all." At least not entirely. She uttered a heavy sigh. They were her friends, so she brushed aside her pride and told them about her disappointment at the bank. And because they were her friends, they offered commiseration and support and another round of shots.

Fiona squeezed her hand. "I'm sorry."

But it was clear she understood why the loan had been refused. Serena understood, too. But it had been her last hope to pay off the lawsuit without having to sell the house.

"Maybe I should have seduced Gordon," she said to Fiona. Maybe he would have given her the loan, then. He'd made it very clear that he was still interested in *her*. Just not in her business.

Fiona laughed.

"It'd make more sense than seducing Cody," she said.

Tammy snorted wine out of her nose. "What? *You* tried to seduce Cody?"

"Fiona told me to," Serena said.

"Why?" Tammy asked.

"So he wouldn't sue me."

"Why are you so worried about that?" Tammy asked. She told her about his slipping in the bathtub.

"You saw him naked?" Tammy asked dreamily.

Heat rushed to Serena's face, and she could only nod as her throat closed up with remembered desire.

Tammy waved her hand in front of her face, as if she were imagining it, too. "That explains why you would think about it. But I figured he'd already be in your bed by now."

His dog occasionally was. But not him. "He's not my type," Serena said. She'd been saying that a lot lately.

"A man that good-looking is every woman's type," Tammy said.

Fiona laughed. "Not Serena. She needs a more serious guy. She needs someone like Braden."

"She needs another drink," Serena answered for herself as she got the waitress's attention this time. She didn't need the drink because she could already feel the alcohol in the warmth of her blood. But she'd make do with it since she couldn't have what she really wanted. The loan.

Not Cody.

8

"SINCE WHEN DO YOU not want to go to the bar?" Wyatt asked Cody as he held open the Filling Station door for him.

Since he had someplace he would rather be—at the house with Serena, making sure she was all right. Was that her he'd seen earlier leaving the bank? And if so, why had she looked so upset? What was going on with her?

"Remember he has a concussion," Dawson said. He was behind Cody, nudging him through the door. "It can affect someone's personality."

Maybe that was his problem. But he hadn't been able to get Serena off his mind even before he'd hit his head. She was so damn sexy with that hair and her body...

And...

Even now—in the crowded bar—he thought he could hear her laugh, which was ridiculous given how sad she'd looked earlier. But had that been her then? He'd been three floors above her and hadn't gotten a good look at her face. Maybe he'd just imagined it had been her on the street, too, like he imagined her in his bed every night.

"The girls have our booth," Wyatt said.

"We can sit somewhere else," Braden said as he followed Dawson. Wyatt had insisted on their boss coming along to the bar, too. Since Braden's divorce, Wyatt had made it his mission to keep him from brooding alone in his office.

"No, we can make room," Wyatt assured him. "Fiona can sit on my lap."

Cody glanced toward their usual booth at the back of the bar near the pool tables. And his heart stopped for just a moment when he saw Serena there, her head thrown back as she laughed.

He hadn't been mistaken; he had heard her—that distinctive, husky, sexy-as-sin laugh of hers. She was here with Fiona and Tammy.

"And Serena can sit on yours," Wyatt continued.

Cody liked that image—of Serena's sexy tush pressed against his groin, her hair tickling his face and his throat as she leaned back against him—grinding her hips against his. Then he realized Wyatt hadn't been talking to him; he was talking to Braden.

Their superintendent nervously chuckled. "Another one of Fiona's wild friends?"

"No!" Cody said. Serena wasn't wild; she was sweet and serious.

And based on her flushed face and bright eyes, it looked like she was slightly tipsy now. Or maybe even more than slightly…

He had never seen her drink anything stronger than iced tea at the house.

Wyatt chuckled. "I figured you wouldn't get anywhere with her. Serena's too smart to fall for your flirting."

She was.

"So she's smart and beautiful," Braden mused as he stared at her with obvious interest.

"I think you two would have a lot in common," Wyatt told him.

Cody's stomach lurched as he realized Wyatt was right. Serena was a lot like Braden; she took responsibility for everyone, even him. She took care of people.

"I don't think she's looking to get involved with anyone right now," Cody cautioned them.

Wyatt laughed. "Just because she turned you down flat doesn't mean she doesn't want to date a nice guy."

But she hadn't dated anyone as long as he'd been living there. And Stanley, who shared everything he observed, had said he hadn't seen her go out with anyone either.

The kid had wondered why. He obviously had a crush on her, too. *Too?* Did Cody? Was that what this was? A crush like he used to get on teachers who'd been nice to him? He'd gotten over them quickly enough when he'd been moved to another foster home and another school.

He would get over Serena, too, when he moved out to Washington to become a smoke jumper. He had every intention of applying for that position and following his plan. Nothing had changed for him.

He shrugged. "Whatever," he said. "I just didn't want to see the old guy get shot down."

Braden wasn't really old, probably just a few years over thirty. But he seemed older—at least to Cody, who wanted nothing to do with being responsible for anyone else.

Braden snorted. "I'll be fine," he said. "In fact it may surprise you how much game this *old guy* actually has."

Cody should have been happy to see his boss like this after how devastated he'd been following his divorce. Wyatt, who slung his arm across Braden's shoulders and steered him toward the booth, was obviously thrilled.

Cody couldn't have been less so. He didn't want to watch a man he liked and respected hit on a woman he wanted. He'd barely been able to admit it to himself, so he couldn't say it aloud, especially not in front of Wyatt and Dawson who would consider this poetic justice for all the times Cody had hit on their women.

Maybe he should rename Annie and call her Karma—since it was such a bitch.

Fiona had been right. Braden Zimmer was a very nice man. He was also good-looking with his short brown hair and serious brown eyes.

But he wasn't Cody. Cody was the man Serena couldn't stop staring at. He sat at the end of the booth, in a chair he'd pulled up to the table. He was quiet, almost like he was brooding. She wasn't the only one who'd noticed.

"What's wrong with you?" Wyatt asked. "You finally realize you have no chance of stealing my woman?"

Cody chuckled, but it sounded forced—at least to Serena. "Thought I'd lull you into a false sense of security for a while," Cody told him. Then he wiggled his dark blond brows over green eyes that twinkled with wickedness. "I'll wait until her bachelorette party to have my way with her."

Tammy giggled. "The only way you're attending that party is as the entertainment," she said. "You can be the stripper."

"What would be the point?" Wyatt asked. "Everybody's already seen him naked."

"Especially after his little bathtub incident," Dawson said. "Glad I'm not taking EMT calls anymore. Poor Owen."

Wyatt snorted with mock-disgust. "The whole thing was probably staged just to get attention."

Serena had briefly entertained that idea—before she'd realized he was actually hurt. But it had already been too late then. She'd seen him in all his naked glory, and she couldn't get that image out of her mind.

"Hey, I'm not the one who got mistaken for a male stripper," Cody said with a pointed stare at Wyatt.

Wyatt raised his hands defensively. "That wasn't me—that was the boss. I had to defend him from a bunch of drunk women during male stripper night at that new club in town."

"Exotic dancer," Braden corrected them with feigned snootiness. "I was mistaken for an exotic dancer."

In addition to being good-looking, he was funny and charming, too. What was wrong with her? Why wasn't she attracted to him? He was sitting close to Serena, but

he wasn't making her pulse quicken or her skin tingle—
not like Cody did with just a glance.

"There's your entertainment," Cody told Tammy.

She shook her head. "Then I guess you're not getting into the party. The only males allowed will be taking it *all* off."

At the thought of Cody stripping off his clothes, heat
flooded Serena. Crammed into one side of the booth
between Braden and Dawson, she struggled to draw a
deep breath. But she couldn't get any air.

"Are you okay?" Braden asked her.

"I think I need to leave," she murmured.

She'd had too much to drink—which wasn't much.
A couple of shots and a glass of wine over a couple of
hours. But she had always been a lightweight; that was
why she didn't go out very often.

That and the fact that she needed to be home for
her boarders. She wouldn't have gone out today if she
hadn't hired a home health aide to come in for Mrs.
Gulliver and Mr. Stehouwer. She wouldn't have dared
to leave them alone. The aide would make sure they
were cared for, and the stew she'd left in the crockpot
would feed Stanley and Mr. Tremont, if he came home.
She'd thought she'd seen him a little earlier in the bar.
So maybe he'd eaten here.

"Can you drive her home?" Fiona asked Braden.
"You should see her house. It used to be a stagecoach
stop. It has a porch that wraps around the first floor and
a balcony that wraps around the second story."

Serena wished she was out on the porch now—where
she could breathe. It wasn't just the alcohol or Cody

that was affecting her. The very real possibility that she would be forced to sell the house was making her panic.

Fortunately Dawson slid out of the booth so she could move. But as she slipped out, she teetered on her heels. Dressing up had been a waste of time. Gordon hadn't been impressed with her business attire or her acumen. *Your tenants don't even sign leases, Serena. You have no guarantee how long they will stay.*

Cody had already warned her that he wasn't staying. But he was there for her now; he was the one who wound an arm around her waist and steadied her.

In addition to the physical support, he gave her that fluttery feeling again—that unique, pulse-tripping, skin-tingling sensation.

"It would be stupid for Braden to drive all those miles out of his way," Cody said, "when Serena and I are going to the same house."

Braden had followed her out of the booth. "It's no trouble," he chivalrously insisted. "I would love to see her house."

"It'll be dark soon," Cody said.

Serena had no idea what time it actually was. She'd come straight to the bar after her late afternoon meeting had gone so wrong.

"And with the woods all around it," Cody continued discouragingly, "you wouldn't see much of the house at night. It would be stupid to try now." He sounded almost surly. Why was he talking to his boss that way?

She glanced up at him and found his focus on her face. There was concern in his green eyes. Was he worried that she'd had too much to drink and Braden might take advantage of her? She doubted that; his boss seemed too nice for that.

Now, Cody…

She shivered at the thought of his taking advantage of her—and how much she would undoubtedly enjoy it.

She turned back to Braden. "Thank you," she said. "It was nice meeting you. But Cody's right. We are going to the same house. It makes the most sense for me to ride with him."

"You don't usually leave this early, though," Wyatt remarked to him.

Cody touched the puckered wound on his forehead. "Aftereffects of the concussion."

"Are you sure you should be driving then?" Fiona persisted.

She and Wyatt obviously wanted Braden to bring her home. Apparently they had become one of those couples who were so disgustingly happy they had decided to play Cupid for their friends.

At the moment Serena didn't care; she just wanted to leave. She wanted to go home and enjoy her house while she still had it.

"I'm medically cleared to drive," Cody said. "I'm just tired."

So was Serena. "I'm tired, too," she murmured. "I'm sorry. I'd just really like to go home. Now."

Cody didn't wait for the others to agree. He began to steer her through the crowded bar.

"It was nice meeting you," Braden called after her.

She turned back and waved at him. He looked disappointed, like Gordon had looked when she'd turned down his offer to go out to dinner that evening. He hadn't understood that she might not want to eat with him after he'd crushed all her hopes and dreams.

Cody's arm tightened around her waist as he guided her over the peanuts and around the other patrons. His hip bumped against hers; his thigh rubbed against her.

She giggled.

"What's so funny?" Cody asked.

"I have two really nice guys interested in me," she said. "But I'm going home with *you*."

"You don't think I'm a nice guy?" he asked as he led her out the back door to the parking lot.

Due to cold winters and hot summers, the asphalt had buckled. Her heel got stuck in a crack, and she nearly fell. She would have—if his arm hadn't tightened around her even more.

"I think you can be kind," she said. What he was doing for Stanley was very generous. "But you're not a nice guy in the way that Braden and Gordon Townsend are."

"Who the hell is Gordon Townsend?"

She wasn't about to talk about the bank officer, so she just shook her head, which was already light from the alcohol. She swayed again, and her legs threatened to fold beneath her.

Maybe Cody was sick of trying to hold her upright because he just lifted her, as if she truly was a light weight. Fortunately he didn't sling her over his shoulder, fireman-style, or she might have hurled. One arm beneath her knees and the other around her back, he cradled her against his chest.

She was tired and a little drunk, so she laid her head on his shoulder. She wished she could rest all her burdens there. His shoulders were wide enough to carry them. But he wasn't the kind of guy she could count on to be there for her.

So why was he the man she'd wanted to go home with?

9

SERENA DIDN'T THINK he was nice like Braden or Gordon Townsend—whoever the hell he was. Cody hadn't recognized the name.

Nor had he recognized all the emotions he'd experienced that night. Had that been jealousy nagging at him when he'd had to watch his boss flirt with her?

And what was he feeling now as he glanced across his truck console to the passenger seat, where she'd fallen asleep? Something shifted in his chest.

Was this protectiveness?

Of course firefighters were protective. That was part of their job description—to save people and property from destruction. It wasn't personal.

But with Serena it felt different. She hadn't just had too much to drink tonight. Something else was going on with her—something that made her cry outside the bank. He knew now that it had been her he'd seen from the conference room window. And beneath her forced smile at the bar, he'd seen her sadness and her anxiety. Something was bothering her.

He intended to find out what. He opened his door

and walked around the front of the truck to open hers. The seat belt held her from falling out; her limp body dangled over it. He unclasped the belt and caught her.

Like she had in the parking lot, she automatically moved her head to the crook of his neck. Her warm breath tickled his throat, making his skin tingle. The excitement he should have felt earlier—at the prospect of traveling to fight a wildfire and especially at the opportunity to become a smoke jumper—he felt now instead. It surged through his body, tensing his muscles and hardening his cock. His erection strained against the fly of his pants.

What was it about Serena Beaumont that affected him so much? She was beautiful but in a natural way that he usually found too tame for his taste. She didn't wear a lot of makeup. Her lashes were probably that long and black without mascara, her lips normally that pink. And he suspected she'd been born with her tan.

But it wasn't just that she was physically beautiful. Her beauty went deeper than her skin. It was in the gentle way she treated her elderly boarders and in her patience with the overly energetic puppy. She'd quickly housebroken Annie. Cody was afraid she might housebreak him, too.

She wasn't just making his skin tingle; she was getting under it in a way no other woman ever had. And he hadn't even made love to her. He'd only kissed her.

Her lips grazed his neck as she shifted in his arms. Then she murmured his name, "Cody…"

And his pulse quickened even more. "Shh…"

It was better that she stay sleeping; then he would be able to resist temptation.

He wanted to be a good guy for her. He carried her up the wide steps of the front porch. Even though night had fallen, only the screen door was shut, and there was no lock on it. The door with the dead bolt wasn't even closed. Anyone could walk right in and maybe had the night his bathtub had been greased up.

He didn't have to juggle her to open the screen door; it pushed out as Annie stepped onto the porch. So much for her staying out of the common areas of the house.

But she hadn't piddled on any floors or eaten any antiques. Like him, she must have wanted to be good for Serena. Annie sniffed Serena's dangling hand and Cody's. Serena's other arm was around his shoulders, her fingers clutching his shirt even as she slept.

Cody stepped through the door Annie had opened, but the dog didn't come back inside the house. She lifted her head and peered around the darkness as if looking at something he couldn't see. But he felt that odd sensation Dawson had mentioned feeling when the arsonist had been stalking his girlfriend, the reporter Avery Kincaid. He felt like he was being watched.

"Is there anyone out there, girl?" he asked the dog.

Annie stepped off the porch and lifted her head to sniff the air. Only a slight breeze blew, rustling the leaves in the trees.

Serena shifted against him, her lips brushing his throat again as she murmured, "Who?"

That was what he'd like to know. Was there someone out there? The arsonist?

But he wouldn't have bothered greasing up a bathtub; he would have burned down the house instead.

"Get 'im, girl," he told Annie as she bounded down the porch steps and ran into the darkness. She was probably chasing a raccoon or a possum—whatever critters wandered the woods at night. But he felt a little better that she'd gone off to investigate as he closed and locked both doors behind them.

The old folks were home. So was Stanley. His beat-up Pontiac was parked alongside one curve of the circular driveway. Cody didn't know about the other boarder; he'd barely seen Mr. Tremont. They had just passed in the hall one morning. Tremont was older than Cody with hair grayer than Mr. Stehouwer's. But he was probably only in his forties. He was really fit but for a slight limp.

If Mr. Tremont wasn't home, he better have taken his key when he'd left. Or he wouldn't be getting back inside the house.

Cody tightened his arms around Serena as he considered how long she'd been living with her doors unlocked—with the possibility of any danger sneaking into her house, into her bed.

He carried her up to her apartment on the third floor. Of course the door wasn't locked; it wasn't even shut. For an attic it had high ceilings, and the dormer windows let in considerable moonlight—enough that he easily found her brass bed—piled high with pillows—against the gable wall.

As he laid her on the mattress, the moonlight illuminated her beautiful face. Her lashes—so long and dark—lay against her cheeks. But then they fluttered and her eyes opened.

She stared up at him in surprise. "What are you doing in my bedroom?"

He could have told her the truth. He could have told her that he was being a good guy. Instead he told her what she and everyone else expected of him. "I'm seducing you," he said.

She shook her head. "I'm supposed to do that to you."

He laughed; she was more drunk than he'd thought. But then he remembered her friend's crazy suggestion. "That's right. You're supposed to seduce *me*. So I won't sue you, which I never considered doing for a second."

She reached up and gently traced the ridge of his stitches. "But you were hurt on my property…"

"I'm fine."

Her fingers stroked the side of his face and trailed along his jaw. "Yes, you are…"

"So I'm not going to sue you," he assured her.

"That's good," she said. "I already have one lawsuit against me."

"Someone's suing you?" Maybe that explained her sadness. "Who?" He would hurt that person—badly— or at least reason with him. No matter what had happened Serena didn't deserve to be sued.

She skimmed her fingers over his lips now and murmured, "Shh…"

"We'll talk tomorrow," he agreed. "After you've had some sleep…" *And a chance to sober up.*

"I don't want to talk." She reached up and locked her arms around his neck—then she pulled him down on top of her. "I just want you." Her lips replaced her fingers as she kissed him.

His body had already been aching for hers. He wanted her so badly. But not like this.

He pulled back. "Serena…"

She was awake now, her hands tugging at his shirt and then his belt. Before he could stop her, she pulled it free of his pants. The buckle hit the floor with a clank, and she giggled. Then she reached for the button at his waist.

He sucked in a breath as her fingers dipped inside his fly. His erection throbbed. Did he possess enough willpower to control his desire?

Especially with her touching him…

"Serena, we can't do this."

"I know you're not sticking around," she said. "I know you're not my type. I know you're not a good guy…"

"Then why do you want me?" he wondered aloud.

She giggled again. "Because you're hot." She reached for the buttons on her blouse. "I'm hot, too," she murmured.

His breath escaped in a gasp as she parted her blouse and shrugged it off. Her bra was lace, the cups barely big enough to contain her round breasts. "You're very hot…"

"It's sweltering up here," she said.

He hadn't noticed the heat. He hadn't noticed anything but how beautiful she was. She wriggled out of her skirt, so that she wore only the bra and matching lace panties.

His heart pounded frantically; he'd never wanted anyone more. When she reached for him again, tugging on his shirt, he wasn't sure how he would resist her or if he could…

HER HEAD POUNDING, Serena squinted against the light streaming through the window over her bed. Had she slipped in the bathtub? Did *she* have a concussion now?

Her head hurt so badly, and she couldn't remember what had happened the night before. She'd gone to the bank in the afternoon. Gordon had given her bad news. Then she'd met her friends at the bar.

And some nice man named Braden.

Had she…?

She lifted the thin sheet covering her and saw that she wore only her panties. Her bra lay beside the bed, tangled around a man's belt. A man's shirt covered her blouse and skirt.

Heat rushed to her face. She had been with someone. Who? She'd talked to Gordon. And then Braden.

But she hadn't wanted either of them. She'd wanted Cody, his strong arms locked around her. A memory flashed through her mind of him carrying her.

She hadn't even been able to walk on her own. She couldn't drink. She wouldn't drink. Never again. Because what had happened after he'd carried her up to bed?

What had she done?

She heard wood creaking as someone climbed the stairs and crossed the attic floor. She squeezed her eyes shut again—not because of the brightness of the sun but because of embarrassment. She didn't want to face him or what she'd done.

And her biggest regret wasn't that she'd done it, but that she couldn't even remember it.

"Wake up, sleepyhead," a deep voice murmured. "I brought you coffee."

She could smell the richness of it with just a hint of cinnamon—the way she always made it. Her nose wrinkled, and her mouth began to water. She needed that coffee.

But she needed to maintain whatever dignity she had left as well. So she kept her eyes closed.

A big hand folded over hers, gently prying her fingers from the edge of the sheet she'd pulled back up. He'd already seen her like this—already seen her breasts, touched them, tasted them…

So she shouldn't have been shy, but she struggled to hold the sheet. He chuckled.

"I also brought you aspirin," he said. And he dropped the pills into her hand.

She opened her eyes, stared down at the pills and then glanced up at his grinning face. He looked so damn happy and refreshed—like he'd slept well, like he wasn't hungover. But then he wasn't. She couldn't remember if he'd even had anything to drink at the bar.

He picked up a glass of water from the tray he'd placed next to her bed—the tray that held a mug of steaming coffee and a plate of toast. "Take the aspirin," he told her.

Her head pounded too much for her to protest. She

swallowed them with a sip of the water. Then she reached for the coffee. "You made this?"

He nodded. "I have skills," he bragged. "But then you know that…"

What skills had he used last night that she couldn't remember? Her skin flushed again—maybe it was because of the coffee. Or maybe it was because of him. He sat on the bed next to her, his chest bare but for a light dusting of golden hair. At least he wore pants, but the top button was undone so that they rode low on his lean hips.

"But you put me to shame last night," he said. "The things you did to me…"

Serena groaned. What had she done?

He'd carried her upstairs. And she'd kissed him. She winced again as she remembered pulling off his belt and his shirt.

Then her own clothes…

"I had no idea you were so wild," Cody said. "You couldn't get enough of me."

She could understand that. It had been a while since she'd been with anyone. And she'd never been with anyone like Cody. She wanted to make love with him now so that she would know how it felt…

"The way you clawed my back…" he said, whistling between his teeth. "And bit my neck…"

She narrowed her eyes and studied him. The only marks that she could see on his body were the stitches on his forehead. "Are you messing with me?"

"Hey," he said. "You're the one who insisted on seducing me."

Her face heated; she remembered saying that and being the aggressor. He'd tried to stop her.

But if they had had sex…

She must have seduced him.

10

CODY TOUCHED HER flushed cheek. "You have no reason to be embarrassed," he told her.

She grimaced. "Yes, I do. I got drunk and threw myself at you."

"Yes."

She pulled the sheet over her face. "I'm sorry," she said, her voice muffled. "I'm your landlady. I understand if you can't stay here anymore."

"Nothing happened," he told her.

"What?"

He reached for the sheet and tugged. It slipped a little lower so that it barely covered the tops of her bare breasts.

"Nothing happened," he repeated. But he wasn't certain how he had summoned the willpower to resist her.

He still wanted her.

His body throbbed, his every muscle tense and aching with needing her.

"Really?" she asked, clearly skeptical of his claim.

"I know you don't think I'm a good guy," he said.

"But I'm not a creep either. You were drunk, so I wouldn't take advantage of you."

She stared up at him in the way that unnerved him so much. "You are a good guy."

He shook his head. "No. I'm just not a creep."

"You didn't have sex with me," she said. "Even though I threw myself at you."

"You didn't claw or bite me," he said. "I was only teasing."

"But I undressed you and myself…"

He groaned as he remembered her fingers caressing his skin. "You did do that."

"But nothing happened…"

"No," he regretfully told her.

"And you still made me breakfast and brought me aspirin."

He shook his head. "It's not a big deal." He didn't want her gratitude. He'd done what she would have for any of her boarders. But unlike Serena, who did everything out of the kindness of her heart, he had ulterior motives.

"It is to me," she said. "Thank you."

He wasn't sure if she was thanking him for not taking advantage or for the coffee and aspirin. "You're welcome."

"I don't know why you don't want anyone else to know what a good guy you really are."

He trailed his fingers along her jaw and tipped her chin. Her eyes were clear, no redness around the dark irises, as she stared up at him.

"What?" she asked.

"Are you completely sober?"

She nodded.

"Your head's not hurting anymore?"

"No."

He lowered his mouth to hers. He kissed her like he'd wanted to kiss her last night—deeply, passionately. When he pulled away, she was panting for breath. "I'm not a good guy," he said. "Not anymore…"

And he pulled the sheet from her body.

SERENA SHIVERED—not because she was cold but because of the way Cody stared at her. His gaze was like a caress; she could feel it sliding over her skin. Her nipples tightened, begging for his touch. She needed his hands on her—his mouth.

But he stood up. Maybe he was having second thoughts and had remembered they'd agreed sleeping together would be a bad idea. She didn't want to think about that right now.

"Cody…" She reached out for him.

But he stood firm. Then he jerked down his zipper and kicked off his pants and his boxers along with them. And he was naked—gloriously naked like he'd been the night she'd found him in the bathroom.

She hadn't been able to get that image out of her mind or stop wanting him. Maybe sleeping with him would assuage that desire so she could focus again. "Cody…"

He didn't crawl back into bed with her. He leaned over her instead, skimming his fingertips along her shoulders and then over her breasts. He touched her nipples, and she shifted against the mattress.

She needed him. She lifted her arms, reaching up for him. But he held back.

He trailed his fingers down her stomach and over the core of her. Through the lace he stroked her.

She squirmed as a pressure built, demanding release.

He hooked a finger in the lace and tugged the panties down her legs. Then finally he joined her in the bed—but only partially. His legs hung off the end of the mattress as he lifted her legs and hooked them over his shoulders. Then his lips moved over her like his fingers had. He teased her clit with his tongue.

She ran her fingers through his hair and then down to his shoulders, clutching at them and trying to drag him up. He was driving her crazy. She wanted him inside, filling her. But then his tongue was there, sliding in and out. His hands moved up her body, and he took her nipples between the tips of his fingers—rolling and teasing them.

Her need for release intensified until she thought it might tear her apart. She reached up and wrapped her hands around the bars in the brass headboard, grasping tightly as he continued to sensually torment her to madness.

Then his tongue flicked over her clit before he closed his lips over and suckled it. One of his hands moved from her breasts, and he drove a finger—then two—inside her.

Finally the pressure—the intolerable pressure—

broke. She cried out. And her body shuddered with the orgasmic release.

She lay limply against the mattress. He was good. So good…

She wanted to be good to him, too. So she summoned her strength and pulled him onto the bed with her. Then she pushed him onto his back. She moved her mouth over him, sliding her lips up and down the impressive, pulsing length of his erection.

His fingers moved through her tangled hair. "Serena…" But he didn't come. Instead he pulled her up his body, her breasts brushing over his chest. That golden hair raised her nipples into tight buds again. He kissed her, his lips moving over hers—his teeth nibbling gently. Then his tongue flicked out, sliding over her lip as if to soothe the hurt. But he hadn't hurt her.

She stroked his tongue with hers. They tangled. The kiss was hot and wet and as wild as he made her feel. And as he kissed her, he touched her—everywhere. His hands slid over her ass, cupping her buttocks. Then he moved a finger between her legs and stroked the core of her.

She gasped for breath as desire overwhelmed her again. Her heart pounded frantically. Despite the pleasure he'd already given her, she was greedy, desperate, for more. For him…

"I want you," she murmured. "I want you inside me…"

He groaned. But instead of sliding into her, he pulled away—leaning out of the bed. Then he held up a condom.

She took it from his hand and tore open the packet with her teeth. Then she rolled it over him, her hand pumping him through the latex.

He groaned again. "If you keep touching me like that, I'm not going to last."

Gently he pushed her onto her back. Then his body covered hers, and he nudged between her legs. She was wet and ready for him—her body already pulsing with her desperate need for another release. She parted her legs and arched as his cock slowly entered her. He was so big. So long...

He filled her. And then some.

Her body shuddered at the sensation—at the completeness she felt. Until he'd filled her, she hadn't realized she'd been empty. Now she was full. But it wasn't enough for him to just be inside her. She shifted beneath him, wanting more.

So he moved. He stroked in and out of her, driving deep. Then he pulled out and started all over again. She lifted her legs and locked them around his waist. And she grasped his broad shoulders.

He lowered his head and kissed her. She arched against him, rubbing her breasts over his chest. Then she raked her nails lightly down his back.

He shuddered. "Serena..."

She nipped his bottom lip. "You accused me of clawing and biting," she reminded him.

"You're wild," he agreed. Then he reached between their bodies and stroked her clit.

And she went wild in his arms. She bucked and

writhed, fighting for the release she needed. The pressure was wound so tightly inside her.

"You're driving me crazy," she told him.

He nipped her bottom lip—then the side of her neck. Then he hunched his back and lowered his head to pull a nipple into his mouth. All the while, he thrust his hips and continued to drive her crazy with the seductive rhythm.

She came apart in his arms—the intensity of the second orgasm overwhelming her. She'd never felt anything so fiercely. She cried out. But his mouth was there swallowing her cry. Then his body tensed and shuddered as he came.

They lay, tangled together on the bed, for several long moments before he moved. He slipped away for just a few minutes, long enough to clean up in her bathroom.

He pulled her into his arms, holding her against his chest. Like hers, it rose and fell with his struggle to regain his breath.

"Wow," she murmured between pants. She knew now how he'd earned the reputation he had. He was an amazing lover.

But she'd actually never heard anyone say what kind of lover he was—just what a flirt. Was he like Tammy? All talk and no action? No. He definitely knew how to make love so that she couldn't think, couldn't feel anything but pleasure.

Making love with him hadn't been a bad idea. Falling for him would be, though. So she would make certain that wouldn't happen. She would only use him to distract herself from her other problems.

Which he had. Very well.

"Thank you," she said.

"You already thanked me," he reminded her.

"I thanked you for bringing me home last night," she said. "For not taking advantage of my drunkenness."

"Why were you drinking?" he asked. "Seems out of character for you."

She was glad he knew it wasn't something she did often.

"Did it have anything to do with what happened at the bank?" he asked.

She tensed. "How do you know about that?" Wasn't that all supposed to be confidential? "Do you know Gordon Townsend?"

He tensed now, and there was a strange harshness in his voice when he replied, "You mentioned him last night, but I have no idea who that is."

"Gordon is one of the loan officers."

"You were applying for a loan?"

She nodded.

"Why? I thought you inherited this house from your mom. Did she have a mortgage on it?"

"No." Her great-great-grandfather had built it himself before mortgages even existed. As far as she knew there had never been one on it.

"Then why do you need one?" he asked. "To pay the lawsuit?"

"You know about that, too?" she asked.

"You told me last night."

She wondered what else she'd said. How sexy he was? How much she wanted him?

"Who sued you?" he asked.

Pain clutched her heart, and she blinked back the tears stinging her eyes. "My twin sister."

His green eyes widened with shock and pleasure. "There are two of you?"

"Don't get any sick fantasies about us," she warned him. "You won't ever see Courtney in Northern Lakes again." Growing up, she'd made no secret of how much she'd hated Northern Lakes—how boring she'd found it—and how she couldn't wait to leave it and never return. "She didn't even come home for Mom's funeral last year."

"I'm sorry," he said, his hand stroking her back soothingly. "So why is she suing you?"

"For half the value of the house."

He nodded in understanding. "That's why you wanted a mortgage."

"Yes." She sighed. "But because of the lawsuit, I can't get one. The settlement is already a lien on the house."

"So you'll have to sell?"

"I can't." She refused to consider it; there had to be another way.

"Why not?" he asked. "It's just a house."

She pulled away from him and sat up, staring down. She was the one shocked now. She'd thought he'd gotten to know her at least a little bit, but apparently only well enough to know she wasn't a drunk. How had she misjudged him so much, too? "How can you say that?"

His broad shoulders moved against the pillows in a

big shrug. "Because it's just a house," he said dismissively. "I lived in a lot of them growing up."

"Your family moved a lot?" She couldn't imagine it. She'd even hated going away to college. But she'd had no choice once she'd taken all the nursing courses the community college had offered. She'd left for a little while, but she hadn't been able to stay away. She'd been too homesick, so she'd dropped out.

"I didn't have a family," he said. "As a baby, I was left at a firehouse just like Annie was."

Sympathy for him squeezed her heart. He had been abandoned. How could someone have just left him like that?

"I lived in a lot of foster homes for the first eighteen years of my life," he continued.

"You were never adopted?" She couldn't believe that. With as gorgeous a man as he'd become, he must have been an adorable child.

"I was once," he said. "For a couple of years. I guess when I hit my terrible twos, they decided having a kid was too much for them, and they put me back in the system."

So he had been abandoned again. Her heart ached for the pain he must have suffered. "Weren't you adopted again?"

He shook his head. "No. I think that labeled me as a problem child. Hyperactive and attachment disorder or something…"

It sounded like his adoptive parents had had the attachment disorder. How could they have returned a child like they would have clothes they hadn't worn?

"But that was fine. I liked the variety of living in those different foster homes," he said, perhaps a little too emphatically, as if he was trying to convince himself as much as her. "I liked moving to new places, living with different people."

"Really?" she asked doubtfully. It sounded like a nightmare to her.

"Yeah, I would have gotten bored always staying in one place," he said. "That's what I like about being a Hotshot—the travel."

She knew that was part of the job. "You've been in Northern Lakes a lot this summer."

"Because of the arsonist," he said.

"He hasn't set any more fires," she said. At least none that she'd heard about. "Maybe he's stopped…"

"Hopefully," he said, but he sounded doubtful. "I'd hate to leave before he's caught."

She tensed. "Leave?"

"I'm going to be interviewing for another job," he said, "for a smoke jumper position that operates out of a base camp in Washington."

"You would leave the Huron Hotshots." She thought he was close to his coworkers. Even though they relentlessly needled each other, there was also affection apparent between them.

"It's always been my goal to be a smoke jumper," he said. "I just had to put in a couple of seasons as a Hotshot to get the experience necessary for the position."

She'd been such an idiot for sleeping with him, and she didn't have the excuse of still being drunk. He'd made it clear from the beginning that he wasn't staying. But now that she'd slept with him, she wanted to do it again.

And again…

But that would only put her at greater risk of falling in love with him. And she couldn't do that because then it would break her heart when he left—just like he'd warned her.

She had no one but herself to blame.

11

CODY WASN'T SURE what he'd expected after sleeping with Serena. But he'd at least hoped to do it again. Instead she'd frozen him out. She hadn't let him close to her since that hot, amazing morning when they'd had sex.

That was all it had been. Had she wanted more? Had she thought he'd declare his undying love and stick around—to help her with the house?

He wasn't that kind of guy. As he'd told her, he didn't get why she was so upset about the place. It was just a house, though clearly it meant a lot to her because it had been in her family so long.

But it was also a money pit. Once she'd had the air-conditioning fixed, the roof had started leaking. He wasn't sure why she wanted to hang on to a place that was so old it was falling apart.

She was too young to tie herself down. She hadn't been out since that night she'd gone to the Filling Station.

Of course it had only been a few days. But that seemed like an eternity to him. He had to go to town to get away from her because being around her and not being with her, inside her...

That was driving him crazy. He'd never been so on edge—so achy and needy. He knew now how it could be between them—how wild and wonderful...

So why didn't she want to do it again?

Hadn't she enjoyed it?

Maybe he should have taken more time—given her more orgasms. He could if she gave him another chance. But he was too proud to ask, to force his attention on someone who clearly didn't want it.

Annie begged for attention, bouncing beside him as he walked to his truck. Stanley was already at the firehouse, washing trucks. It was just his summer job until he would start college in the fall. He was working to pay his tuition. Cody would find a way to help him out with what he couldn't afford, just like he'd helped him out with his room and board. Serena had been instrumental in that, though.

She had understood his need to help Stanley, even though Cody wasn't certain he understood it. Maybe it was because when Stanley had come to that last group home Cody felt like a big brother to him.

Yeah, he would find some way to help the kid with tuition—even if he had to force a loan on him. Cody had money. As a Hotshot, he worked crazy overtime. And because the US Forest Service had provided a cabin, he'd had few expenses. Just his truck.

He climbed into it now and slid the key in the ignition. Braden and the assistant superintendents were given US Forest Service trucks to drive, but Cody preferred having his own. He'd put a lift kit on it and jacked it up. With its big tires and clearance, it could get through parts of the forest that the official trucks could not.

Those tires spun in the muddy driveway as he headed away from the house. He'd had enough of Serena's silent treatment. She was clearly mad at him.

That was fine. They would never see eye to eye on the house or his need to travel. So it was good that he would be leaving soon. He just had to check in at the firehouse before taking off to Washington for that interview.

Maybe he should have told her he'd be gone for a while. But she hadn't been receptive to any of his other attempts at conversation.

Or at anything else…

Had she seen him leaving with his bag?

He glanced back at the house. But he couldn't see it through the trees. He could have turned around, gone back and told her.

But instead he revved the engine and tore out of the driveway onto the street, tires squealing and mud flying behind him. He was mad now. He was mad that she was mad.

He'd been straight with her from the beginning. He'd told her that they were a bad idea. But she'd wanted to make love with him. Of course she'd been drunk then. She hadn't turned him down the next morning, though—when she'd sobered up.

Still…

He could have just brought her the coffee and aspirin and left. He was the one who'd initiated the sex, who wanted more.

Hell, he wasn't upset at her. He was disgusted with himself for being such an idiot. He didn't often get mad anymore, not like when he'd been a kid quick to anger. His temper was probably why they'd moved him so often. So he'd learned to control it. For the most part.

But when his temper flared, he felt like that hothead again. His foot pressed harder on the accelerator. He was the teenager who'd driven too fast, too carelessly— who'd wrecked cars.

He eased his foot off as the road curved. He wasn't that hothead anymore. He was older. Wiser.

But the truck didn't slow down. He moved his foot from the accelerator to the brake. But the pedal hit the floor with no resistance—with no effect.

The brakes were gone. And the curve was too sharp for him to maneuver at this speed. He cursed and braced himself for the crash he wouldn't be able to avoid.

Serena cursed herself. She'd been such a bitch to Cody since that morning he'd given her pleasure like she'd never felt before.

It wasn't his fault that he didn't care about the house. He'd never had a home, so how could she expect him to understand and commiserate with her about the possibility of losing hers?

But that wasn't the only reason she'd frozen him out. She hadn't wanted to get used to him being around and making love with her when she knew he wasn't going to stay. But she hadn't expected him to leave so soon.

He'd been carrying his duffel bag with him when he'd left the house.

She always respected her boarders' privacy. But Cody wasn't just a boarder—not after that morning. He was her lover, too. Or he would be if she hadn't been such a bitch. So she ignored her flash of guilt as she reached for the doorknob of his room. She'd brought the key, but she didn't need it. The knob turned easily.

Of course he wouldn't have bothered locking it behind him if he'd moved out. He wouldn't have left anything for anyone to take. Not that he'd brought much stuff with him anyway. He traveled light so he could travel easily.

He'd told her that, too.

She stepped inside the room. The bed wasn't made; the sheets were tangled as if, like she had, he'd struggled to sleep. She had washed her sheets, but she could still smell him in her bed, still feel his arms around her, whenever she tried to sleep.

She could smell him in his room. She found herself picking up his pillow from the floor. She held it against her chest. But it wasn't like holding him.

He'd left some things on the side table. A watch. A phone case. A picture. She picked up the frame and stared at all the smiling faces of the Hotshot team.

Did he really intend to leave them? To leave Northern Lakes?

Probably. But she didn't suspect today was the day. He'd left too much behind—at least for him—to have moved out. He would come back.

Wouldn't he?

He'd left his window open, too—the curtain rustled in the breeze. Once she'd fixed the air conditioner, the heat wave had broken. It had rained, too. Maybe that had cooled down the temperature.

The rain had made the driveway muddy and the roads slick. Through that open window, she heard the sound of a crash—the sickening crunch of metal and the blare of a car horn. It could have been someone else.

But Cody had just left. So she knew it had to be him. As if Annie knew, too, she began to howl. Serena rushed down the stairs and out the front door. Her car was parked where Fiona and Wyatt had left it when they'd driven it back for her a few days ago.

The keys dangled from the ignition. She started the car and tore out of the driveway—just like Cody had moments ago. She should have stopped, grabbed her purse. She didn't care that she didn't have her driver's license, but maybe she would need her phone to call for help.

At least she had a first aid kit in the trunk. She knew to always have that with her. She was afraid she would need it, especially as she turned the corner and saw the crash site. There were no skid marks on the road. It was like he'd just missed the curve and driven off into the trees. The front of the truck was crumpled against the thick trunk of one—steam rising from beneath its hood.

She pulled off to the shoulder of the road and threw open her door. "Cody!"

Was he okay? Could he hear her?

She hurried over to the truck, worried that she would find him slumped over the wheel. Or worse yet, with his head smashed through the broken windshield. His truck was too old to be equipped with air bags. He'd had no protection when he'd hit the tree head-on like he had.

Her heart pounded fast and frantically. She was so scared that she might have lost him. She braced herself before looking through the broken driver's door window. But the truck was empty. His door was crumpled but the passenger door stood open.

"Cody!" she yelled for him again.

He came around the side of the vehicle, blood trickling from his forehead like it had the night she'd found him on the bathroom floor. She reached out for the wound, her fingertips touching a jagged piece of glass. She needed her first aid kit.

But she didn't want to leave his side—not until she was certain he wouldn't pass out. He obviously had another head wound. What about internal injuries?

He could have broken his ribs on the steering wheel; he could have ruptured organs.

"Are you okay?" she anxiously asked him. "Did you lose consciousness?"

Maybe that was why he'd crashed. Maybe he hadn't fully recovered. Maybe he shouldn't have been driving yet.

"No," he said. "I'm fine." He didn't look fine, though. In addition to being bloody, his face was flushed and his green eyes bright with anger.

"What happened?" She hadn't seen any other vehicle, but that didn't mean that someone hadn't driven him off the road. She'd come around these curves a lot of times and nearly struck someone who had veered across the line into her lane. Usually because they had been preoccupied with a phone call or a text message.

A muscle twitched in his cheek as he clenched his jaw. He was very angry.

"What happened?" she asked again.

He nearly spit out the words when he replied, "My brakes went out."

If it had been a mechanical malfunction, she doubted he would be as mad as he was. There was more to the crash than that. But when she pressed him for more details, he only shook his head.

He wasn't going to share with her what he really thought had happened. Maybe it was because he was mad that she hadn't been talking to him. Or maybe it was because he didn't want to scare her.

But it was too late for that.

Serena was terrified because of how she had felt in those moments when she hadn't known whether or not he had survived the crash. She had been more than upset; she'd been devastated.

Despite his warnings, had she already fallen for Cody Mallehan?

12

EVEN A COUPLE of days later and more than half the country away from her, Cody continued to be haunted by Serena's face. He paced across the concrete floor of the old airport hangar, but all he could see was how terrified she had looked when she'd peered inside his truck. Her naturally tanned skin had been pale, her dark eyes wide with fear. She'd been worried about him in a way that Cody couldn't remember anybody else ever having worried about him.

But she was Serena. She cared about everyone. It was just her nature. Even if she had been mad at him, she still cared. She'd even offered to drive him to the airport when he'd told her about his interview.

Had that been to help him out, though? Or because she wanted him gone now?

He couldn't blame her. But she didn't know what he suspected—that someone had cut his brakes. She didn't know his suspicion that the same someone had tampered with his bathtub. He'd told her that he'd accused Stanley of hazing him. But he hadn't told her what he believed now—that the arsonist was trying to take him out.

Of course he had no proof. So he hadn't shared this with her, or with anyone else. Yet.

He shouldn't have left. He should have postponed his interview until he knew what the hell was really going on in Northern Lakes. He shouldn't have left her alone.

But his truck was old. Maybe the brake line had just rotted out. It was possible. Doubtful given the care he'd always taken with the classic Ford. But possible.

He paced the length of the airport hangar. Metal shelves, filled with parachutes and packs of tools and supplies, lined the walls. This was it: the smoke jumpers' base in North Cascades, Washington. This was where it had all begun—where smoke jumping had started. He'd been there before, so maybe that was why he wasn't as excited as he'd been then. He had already built up his hopes once to have them dashed when he'd been deemed not experienced enough to be a jumper.

Mack McRooney was late for their meeting. But that wasn't why Cody paced. He paced because he was waiting for a call. He took out his phone again and glanced at the screen. He had good enough reception that he couldn't have missed it.

Impatience churned in his stomach. How long was it taking the mechanic to get to his truck? Sure, it probably wasn't repairable. He already suspected that much, but that wasn't the news he waited for. The phone vibrated in his hand, and he nearly dropped it as he hurriedly pressed the button to accept the call. "Yes, what did you find out?"

"That was no accident, man." The mechanic's voice shook with the excitement that Cody struggled to feel. "That brake line was sliced clean. Somebody cut it on purpose."

Cody wasn't excited. He was pissed. And scared, not for himself, but for Serena. He'd left her alone in the house she never bothered to lock. He needed to get back to Northern Lakes.

"Do you want me to call the police for you?" the mechanic asked.

"I will," Cody said. He should have at the crash site. Serena had wanted to. But then he'd told her about the interview. Her skin had paled—like it had when she'd walked up to his truck. But she'd agreed that the police might not come out for a single-vehicle accident.

But now he knew it wasn't an accident at all. Someone had deliberately caused him to crash. "Save the brake line for me," he told the mechanic.

"That's about all I can save, man. The truck…"

It was a total loss. Cody was lucky that was all he'd lost. Worse yet, what if Serena had been in the truck with him? He shuddered to think what could have happened to her. What might—if he wasn't home to protect her.

"I'm gonna try to find a front clip for it, but with how old it is, it's hard to find parts for…"

"I know," Cody said. "It's fine."

"Hope you had insurance."

Replacing the truck was the least of his concerns at the moment. "I need to go," Cody said.

He was no longer alone. Mack McRooney—the bald-headed mountain of a man—had joined him in the airport hangar. "Sorry to keep you waiting," he said.

Cody clicked off his phone and slipped it back in his pocket. His hand was shaking slightly—from the confirmation that someone was after him—as he held it out to Mack.

"No need to be nervous," Mack said. "You and I have been through this before. You already know what I'm going to ask you." He pointed at Cody's head. "What the hell happened to you?"

He shook his head. "Nothing I can't handle." He was going to damn well find out who'd been causing his little accidents. But he had a sick feeling that he already knew. The arsonist was targeting him now.

With Cody gone, would he come after him another way? Would he come after the woman who...

What was Serena to him? The woman he'd slept with once, but who'd avoided him since? Maybe she would be safe. Maybe the arsonist wouldn't realize what she meant to Cody—since Cody wasn't even sure what she meant to him.

Too much...

She meant too much.

"So has Braden called you?" Fiona asked as she leaned over the island in Serena's kitchen.

Serena didn't look up; she focused on the carrots she chopped on the butcher-block cutting board. In high school shop class, she'd made the board for her mother, who'd treasured it like one of the many antiques in the house. "Braden?"

"Braden Zimmer," Fiona said. "Wyatt's boss. You two seemed to hit it off the other night. I wish Cody would have let *him* drive you home."

She was glad he hadn't. She had made enough of a fool of herself with Cody. But he hadn't seemed to mind. He had taken care of her that night. And then the next morning, he'd *really* taken care of her.

Her skin tingled and heated as she remembered the way he'd touched her, the way he'd kissed her…

She had relived over and over again the sensation of his tongue inside her and then his cock…

She had never had orgasms as powerful as the ones he'd given her. Her body felt hot and achy with need for more. For Cody…

"Yeah," Fiona said. "Braden should have driven you home."

"It would have been out of his way," Serena said.

"I don't think he would have minded," Tammy said as she joined them in the kitchen. She'd just finished putting the purple streaks in Mrs. Gulliver's hair and helping her back to her room. "He seemed to really like you."

She shrugged. "I don't know." Mostly because she didn't remember anything but Cody. She couldn't get him out of her mind. She kept thinking about how thoroughly he'd made love to her. And she kept thinking about the other morning when he'd crashed into that tree.

"Trust me," Fiona said. "Braden likes you. And that's huge after what he's been through."

"What's that?"

Had he grown up like Cody had—in a series of foster homes, never staying anyplace for long? Her heart ached for Cody's horrible childhood and his lack of stability. Serena hadn't had a father, but she'd been lucky to have an amazing mother, grandmother and extended family.

"Braden just survived a particularly nasty divorce," Fiona said. "His wife—ex-wife—cheated on him, left him for that man and then heartlessly invited him to attend their wedding."

Tammy cussed. "What a bitch!"

At Tammy's shrill outburst, Annie lifted her head from her paws. She was sprawled at Serena's feet—as usual. Drool had pooled onto the hardwood floor beneath her jowls. Serena really hadn't intended to let the dog into the house. But she'd fallen for Annie like she was afraid she was falling for Cody.

"I wasn't talking about you," Tammy told the dog. "You're not a bitch—at least not like Braden's ex is."

"So has he called you?" Fiona persisted.

Serena shook her head. "But then I didn't give him my number." At least she didn't think she had. Parts of that night were particularly fuzzy—like how her bra had wound up on the floor. She remembered taking off Cody's belt and shirt and her blouse and skirt. But the bra…

"I gave him your number," Fiona said. "And I told him to call you."

Irritation made Serena's voice a little sharp when she replied, "You shouldn't have done that."

"Why not?" Fiona obviously couldn't see the problem. "He's a really nice guy."

"I have another really nice guy who wants to go out with me, too." Gordon had called; he'd wanted to make certain that turning her down for a loan hadn't ruined his chances of dating her.

"Cody?" Tammy snorted. "He's not a nice guy."

"Yes, he is," she defended him.

"He's Cody the Cad," Tammy said. "You can't trust a player like him."

Serena's stomach lurched as a possibility occurred to her. "Were you two ever involved?"

Tammy laughed. "No way. I know better than to flirt with guys like him." She narrowed her eyes and studied Serena's face. "Oh, no…"

"Oh, no, what?" Fiona asked as she looked back and forth between Serena and Tammy. "What happened?"

Serena shook her head. She wasn't about to share what had happened between her and Cody. It wasn't anyone else's business—not even her best friends'. "I don't know what she's talking about."

"You and Cody—something happened," Tammy persisted. "You think he's a nice guy."

She did. But she wasn't going to admit that either. "He's not who I was talking about," she said. "Gordon Townsend has been calling me."

"He turned you down for a loan," Tammy said, as if she needed the reminder.

She was very well aware of that. "Yes, and he feels terrible about it."

"Terrible enough to reconsider?" Tammy wondered.

She hadn't thought about that. But maybe it wouldn't be a bad idea to talk to him again. She had no other choice but to sell the house. While Cody didn't think that would be a big deal, it would destroy her. It would be like losing her mother all over again. She could hear her laugh in this kitchen, hear it echoing off the beams of the adjoining hearth room. When Serena sat on the front porch, sometimes the swing would move as if someone was sitting on it—as if Mama was still there. Or Grandma…

She could feel them all inside this house—all the family who'd lived here before her. And even though Courtney had been gone for years, she could feel her in the house, too—could remember playing with her twin at their mama's feet where Annie was sprawled now.

Would Gordon reconsider and give her a loan?

"I don't know." She doubted that he could, since her circumstances hadn't changed. But maybe he could tell her what she needed to change.

"But he's the reason you don't want to go out with Braden?" Fiona persisted.

She didn't want to go out with Braden because she wasn't interested. Because he didn't make her pulse quicken or her skin tingle…

Gordon didn't do either of those things to her either. Only Cody did…

"I'm sure he's great," Serena replied. "But I have too much going on right now to get involved with anyone."

"Well, I'm glad you weren't calling Cody nice," Tammy said. "I figured you were too smart to fall for his charms."

Apparently she wasn't because she truly believed he was a good guy—even though he didn't want anyone else to know it. Still a little irritated, Serena remarked, "And I figured you would know better than to judge someone by their reputation."

Tammy's face flushed. "Hey…"

But Tammy couldn't deny it. She had a reputation for being a flirt, too. Some people thought she did more than flirt, but they would be wrong. They didn't know Tammy like Serena did. Not that it would matter if she did.

"I know you're mostly just talk," Serena teased her.

Tammy shrugged. "You know me. You don't know Cody."

Serena suspected she knew him better than most people did. She knew about his childhood—or lack of one. And she knew what he did for Stanley even though Stanley didn't know.

"I don't see his truck out front," Tammy said. "He must be out with some woman now."

He was in another state—at a job interview. But since she wasn't certain if anyone else on his Hotshot team was aware of that, she kept her silence. She was getting used to keeping Cody's secrets. The only thing she knew she wouldn't be able to keep was Cody.

He hadn't moved out yet. But he was leaving. Even if he didn't get the smoke jumper job, she doubted he would stick around. Moving was all he knew.

And staying was all she knew. But would she be able to continue living in the house where she'd grown up? Or would she have to sell it to satisfy her sister's lawsuit?

At the moment she was less upset about losing the house than she was at the thought of how close she had come to losing Cody.

If he'd hit that tree a little harder…

He could have been killed. He could have been killed when he'd fallen in the shower, too. Since moving into the boardinghouse, he'd had two really close calls. Was that a coincidence? Or was something else going on?

Was he in danger?

13

CODY WASN'T SURE that coming back to the boarding-house was a good idea. While he'd been worried about Serena, he had to consider that his very presence might put her in danger.

If the arsonist was fixated on him now...

Brady believed that the arsonist was obsessed with the Huron Hotshots team as a whole. He only set the fires when they were in town; he only set fires that could endanger them.

But what if it wasn't the whole team he was after? What if it was only Cody?

Then leaving would make everyone—including Serena—safer. But before he could go, he needed to make certain she was all right. So, the minute his small plane had landed in Northern Lakes, he'd borrowed a US Forest Service truck and headed to the boarding-house. When he'd walked into her kitchen, he had un-wittingly walked into a dangerous situation.

While she had looked relieved to see him, her friends had glared at him. If looks could kill...

Fortunately the other women hadn't stayed long. He watched as their taillights headed down the driveway.

"Did your friends warn you off me again?" Cody asked.

"It's a little late for that."

His heart shifted in his chest. But she couldn't have fallen for him. Since they'd had sex, she'd barely talked to him. "What do you mean?"

"I already slept with you."

"We didn't sleep," he reminded her. But he had an urge to do that—to sleep with her in his arms. Just to keep her safe.

"No," she agreed. "We didn't."

"Did you tell them what happened?"

She arched a dark brow. "Do you think they would have left if I had?"

He chuckled. "Probably not." He patted Annie's head as she nudged his legs. "So why were they glaring at me if they didn't know about us?"

"Because they don't know you."

He chuckled again. "They know me. Everyone does."

She shook her head. "Everyone thinks they do. But they don't have any idea who you really are."

Despite the warm night, his blood chilled. "What do you mean?"

She touched his face, running her fingertips along his jaw. "Don't look so scared," she said. "I won't tell anyone the truth."

"Tell me," he said. "Tell me what you think you know."

"I know you're a good guy," she said. "Even though

you work really hard at keeping that fact from everyone." She rose up on tiptoe and pressed her lips to his.

"What are you doing?" he asked, after her mouth slid away from his.

She stepped back and stared up at him, her eyes wide with feigned innocence—as if she hadn't just kissed him. "I'm taking Annie for a walk."

The dog must have somehow understood her because she headed toward the back door.

"I thought that was Stanley's job," he said.

"Stanley is bowling with Wyatt and Fiona's brother Matt. So I promised I'd take her."

He wasn't sure if she'd promised Stanley or Annie. But he couldn't let her go off alone—not when it would be dark soon. Not with an arsonist potentially lurking around the house. He caught the screen door before it shut and followed Serena and the dog out.

"You don't have to walk with us," she told him. But a little smile played around her mouth. After that kiss, she knew he would follow her. Hell, he would follow her anywhere.

"It's not safe for you to walk alone this close to night," he told her.

She pointed at the overgrown puppy. "I'm not alone. And I know these woods like the back of my hand." She moved sure-footedly over the branches littering the path that wound between trees. "Courtney and I used to play hide-and-seek in them, and flashlight tag."

Most of the foster homes he'd lived in had been in the city, where they'd had to play in the street. That was part of why he'd joined the US Forest Service—for the nature. "It must have been fun growing up here," he said.

"I thought so," she said. "Courtney was bored. She would have rather hung out at the mall."

"There's no mall in Northern Lakes."

She uttered a rueful chuckle. "Exactly. But she was all about fashion and shopping…"

"And you?" he asked, wondering what she'd been like as a child. "What were you about?"

"Learning how to make tea ring like my grandmother."

"Tea ring?"

"The cinnamon-roll thing."

He groaned as he remembered the decadent treat she'd served for brunch. "Tea ring."

"It took years for me to get it right and probably years of patience off her life, standing at the counter with me kneading the dough." She smiled as if the memory touched her.

He had no such sentimental memories. He glanced back at the house behind them. Its windows aglow with lights, it radiated warmth. Like she did…

She slipped her hand into his, and he stared down at their entwined fingers. "This is a bad idea."

Her lips pulled into a slight frown as she acknowledged, "I know."

"Then why?"

"I keep thinking about that accident, about how you could have been hurt so much worse."

He needed to tell her the truth—that it had been no accident. But he didn't want anyone else to overhear him, especially the arsonist. And he didn't know who might be in the woods besides them.

Annie's head was up, her floppy ears almost perked as if she heard something. Then she scampered off ahead of them.

If the arsonist was out there, he was about to be assaulted—by a hundred-plus pounds of affectionate puppy. The dog, her tail wagging, disappeared down the trail.

"So much for walking her," Cody murmured. He stopped in order to turn back.

But Serena tightened her grasp on his hand and tugged him forward. "It's just a little farther," she said.

"What is?"

"The lake."

"There's a lake on your property?"

"This is Northern Lakes. There's a lake on pretty much everyone's property."

"How much land do you own?" he wondered aloud.

"Thirty acres," she said. But her mouth turned down at the corners with a worried frown. She must have been thinking that she might not own it much longer— thanks to her sister.

As a vice tightened around his heart with concern for her, he offered her hand a reassuring squeeze. He could give her more than that, though. He could give her a distraction from her worries for the moment.

"So you're dragging me off into the woods to have your way with me?" he teased.

Her lips curved upward again. "Like I'd have to drag you off into the woods to do that."

"No," he admitted. "No, you wouldn't."

The trees parted at a clearing. And in the middle of the clearing was an expanse of water, the surface rippling and glistening as the sun began to set upon it. Although on their side of the lake the trees were lush and leafy, on the other side they were blackened trunks devoid of all branches.

His breath escaped in a gasp. "The fire came that close?"

She shuddered and nodded. "Yes. If not for the lake…"

It might have taken the house. She could have lost it even before her sister's vindictive lawsuit.

Then she looked up at him. "The lake and you—the Hotshots—stopped it."

For now. But he suspected there would be more fires until they caught the arsonist. He forced a grin. "So how are you going to pay me back? More tea ring?"

She shook her head, her long hair swaying around her body. Then she reached for the bottom of her tank top and peeled it off. It dropped to the ground—followed by her shorts. She stood before him wearing another matching set of lace bra and panties. For such a serious, no-nonsense woman, she liked her sexy underwear, and so did he.

He liked it so much that he couldn't think of anything but getting her out of it. But before he could reach for her, she was reaching for him. She pulled his belt free and tugged down his zipper. His cock—already pulsating with desire for her—sprang free through the fly.

Her fingertips skimmed the tip of it, and he groaned.

He wanted her too much to think about anything but having her. So he pulled his shirt over his head and kicked off his pants until he stood before her entirely naked.

But he didn't feel naked—really naked—until she looked at him that way she always looked at him. How could she see him when no one else ever had?

She dropped to her knees in front of him. Then she closed her hands around him, moving them up and down the length of his cock. As she stroked, she closed her lips around the tip and sucked.

"Serena!" her name tore from his throat as he struggled for control. He had never known a more generous or caring woman.

He clutched her hair—her long, silky hair. Then he tried to pull her to her feet. But she kept driving him crazy with her mouth and hands. Tension filled him, tearing at him. His tenuous grip on her—and on his control—broke. And he shouted her name again as he came.

She stared up at him, her dark eyes bright with passion, as she licked him from her lips. And even though he'd just had a powerful release, need overwhelmed him. He really had never wanted anyone so much that it was almost like a madness.

Was this the arsonist's issue? Was he obsessed with fire the way that Cody was beginning to believe he was obsessed with Serena?

SERENA WATCHED AS Cody's green eyes dilated, turning as dark as hers with desire. He stared at her so intently—

so deeply. There was something more in his gaze than attraction, something that had his brow furrowing almost as if he were confused or troubled.

"What?" she asked, wondering about that look. "What's wrong?"

He shook his head, like he couldn't find the words. "You," he murmured.

It wasn't a compliment, but somehow the way he said it made it sound like one. She smiled. But when he reached for her, she stepped back.

"Serena…" He moved closer.

She turned and leaped into the water. It was too warm to cool her passion for him, which only burned hotter when she heard the splash. But she turned and saw only the wide ripples spreading across the surface of the water.

Where had he gone?

Fingers wrapped around her ankle. And she squealed—just before he tugged her under. Submerged, she blinked and focused on him; gloriously naked, his muscles rippling like the water, he looked like a merman. Some mythical creature sent to lure her to her doom.

But then he released her and she shot to the surface again. She sucked in a breath. And he joined her, tossing back his wet hair. His arms wrapped around her as he kicked his legs, keeping them both afloat. His wet skin pressed against hers.

Then he lowered his head and nipped gently at her bottom lip, catching and holding it between his teeth. His tongue lapped across the fullness, soothing it.

But she wasn't soothed. She was even more aroused, her body burning up with passion. She wanted him so much. She needed him—needed the release he could give her. She linked her arms around his wide shoulders and clung to him.

He moved his mouth from hers, down her throat. As he nibbled on her neck, his hands moved beneath the water. He pushed down the cups of her wet bra. He teased her nipples, rolling them between his fingertips.

She was surprised steam didn't rise from the water as heat flooded her. A moan burned in her throat. One of his hands trailed down her body. Pushing aside her panties he touched her intimately, his fingers moving in and out while his thumb teased her clit.

It wasn't enough; it was too much. The pressure in her body wound tighter—threatening to break her. "Cody…"

She needed more. Then he rocked the pad of his thumb back and forth against her, and she came, screaming his name.

But he wasn't done with her—wasn't done making love to her. He lifted and carried her from the water to the shore where they'd left their clothes. He lowered her down so that she knelt on the mound of garments. And he moved his hand between her legs, driving her into a frenzy again.

She heard foil tear—heard his grunt as he sheathed himself first in latex and then inside her. He thrust deeper, holding her hips against his. His hands moved over her body, cupping her breasts, stroking her clit.

She'd never been loved so thoroughly—so passionately. He nipped at her shoulder then moved his mouth over her cheek until his lips covered hers. She turned and kissed him back. Then she arched to meet his thrusts.

And she came again. Moments later his body shuddered and a guttural cry tore from his throat as he joined her in release. They both fell silent after that, saying nothing to each other as they cleaned up and dressed.

Was he as overwhelmed as she was? Or was he just tired? They linked hands again as they walked back—the lights of the house beckoning to them through the dark woods. When they neared the porch, the screen door pushed open and Annie greeted them. She'd found her way home again—as she always did.

Cody shut both doors and turned the lock. Serena shivered, maybe because her underwear was wet against her skin. Or maybe because of the way Cody had looked when he'd turned that lock, almost as if he thought there was something dangerous outside. Or someone… Was that why he followed her up to the attic?

To protect her? If he really wanted to do that, he would leave her alone so that she didn't get any more attached to him than she already was. Her voice husky, she asked, "How did your interview go?"

Did he get the job? Would he be leaving Northern Lakes soon?

Her question brought a strange look to his handsome face. It was so intense that it was almost frightening. He looked like he had after the accident—angry.

"It didn't go well?" she asked. But how could it have gone well after he'd been in an accident? She touched his head; the fresh wound had already scabbed over. "You should have let me take you to the hospital instead of the airport."

"I didn't want to miss the interview."

"I think he would have understood," she said. "Given that you'd just been in an accident."

"It wasn't an accident," he said.

"But you said your brakes had gone out…"

"It wasn't an accident," he repeated, "because someone cut my brake line. My mechanic confirmed it."

"What are you saying?" she asked. "That someone deliberately tried to hurt you?"

He nodded. "Maybe even kill me."

She shuddered as fear overwhelmed her. She had considered it just moments ago, but that had been just a fleeting consideration because of the coincidences. But she couldn't believe it. Not really.

Things like this didn't happen in Northern Lakes. Nothing dangerous ever happened here—at least until the arsonist had started setting fires.

"Do you think it's him?" she asked. "Do you think the arsonist cut your brake line?"

He nodded. "And maybe tampered with the tub."

"It was so slick…like something had been rubbed over the porcelain," she agreed. "And I washed it earlier that day. It hadn't been like that then."

Then she realized what that meant. "He was here?" she said, and the fear cracked her voice. "He was in my driveway?" And worse yet. "He was in my house?"

She trembled with fear—with the thought of what

could have happened to him or Stanley or Mrs. Gulliver or Mr. Stehouwer or Mr. Tremont.

Cody's arms wrapped around her, stilling her trembling. "It's my fault," he said.

She shook her head. He wasn't the one who'd set the fires. He was the one who'd put them out.

"He's after *me*," Cody said.

Maybe Cody was too close to catching him. But if Cody didn't stop him…

The arsonist might stop Cody. He could have killed him already—nearly had twice. She tensed as fear overwhelmed her.

"Do you want me to leave?" he asked.

"Leave?" she repeated. She wanted him to stay with her and keep her safe. "Why?"

"Because my presence here is putting you in danger."

She hadn't thought about that; she hadn't thought about herself. She could think only about him. About losing him…forever.

14

SHE HADN'T SAID ANYTHING. But her body was stiff in his arms. So Cody asked again, "Do you want me to leave?"

But then he didn't wait for her response. He'd learned too well that it was better to anticipate rejection, then it didn't hurt as bad.

"Of course you do," he said. "And I should."

She shook her head. "No…" But her voice sounded tremulous—uncertain.

"It may not be an issue anyway," he said. "My interview for that jumper position went well. Really well." Which was a lie. He had been distracted—thinking about her, worrying about her. He couldn't even remember what questions Mack had asked him, let alone how he'd answered them. "If I get that job, I won't be stationed out of Northern Lakes anymore."

"You said that." She was still tense—even after their mind-blowing sex.

But he was tense, too. He wanted her again, but even though he held her in his arms, she felt distant from him. Maybe she was anticipating the rejection, too?

"It's based in Washington?" she asked.

"Yes."

"You can't get much farther away than that…"

"No." But would that stop the arsonist? Or would he only turn his sick attention to someone else? And would that be another Hotshot? Or someone else like Serena? Cody didn't know. If he believed—really believed—that the arsonist would leave Northern Lakes alone if he left, he would go immediately, whether he had a job or not.

"What about Stanley?" she asked. "What about Annie?"

A twinge of regret struck his heart. He didn't want to leave the kid. But Stanley had enrolled in the community college close enough to Northern Lakes that he could stay at the boardinghouse with Serena. She would keep an eye on him; she would take care of him like she did everyone else. She would take better care of him than Cody could.

Forcing himself to sound callous, he replied, "They're not my responsibility."

"No, they're not," she readily agreed—too readily. She peered up at him in that way that felt as if she was looking right through him. Then she asked, "So why have you taken responsibility for them?"

His blood chilled and it wasn't because of their damp clothes. "I haven't."

"You've been paying more than half of Stanley's rent," she reminded him. "And you haven't taken Annie back to the humane society."

"They'd put her down. Nobody else would want her."

"You do?"

"No," he said. "But you don't seem to mind her." Just like she didn't seem to mind him and Stanley being around either.

"Annie's a sweet dog," she murmured.

So sweet that she hadn't let out so much as a bark when someone must have been outside tampering with his truck the other night.

"She's not a good watchdog," he pointed out.

Serena sighed. "No. But I wouldn't want a dangerous dog around my boarders."

Her boarders…

He needed to check on them all again. Sure, Mrs. Gulliver and Mr. Stehouwer were too elderly to have climbed the stairs and tampered with his shower. But what about the other boarder? The one who shared the second floor with him and Stanley? The one who was never around.

Cody intended to check him out. Thoroughly.

"What about your boarders?" he asked. "Do you make sure none of them are dangerous before they move in?"

She stiffened again. "Of course I check them out. I do criminal background and credit checks."

"You didn't on me."

"I did when you told me you'd be paying Stanley's rent," she reminded him. "You filled out the application. I checked out both of you."

"So you wouldn't let anyone with a criminal record move in?"

She shook her head. "You're wondering about Mr. Tremont."

"Yes."

"He's a vet," she said.

"Veterinarian?" He had never showed any interest in Annie on the couple of occasions that Cody had run into the gray-haired man.

"Veteran," she corrected. "He was a Marine. I think that might be why he keeps to himself."

Cody nodded and felt a flash of guilt for suspecting the man. He'd already concluded that anyone could have let himself into her unlocked house.

"You need to be more careful," he said.

"I already told you that I do the background checks before anyone moves in."

"You need to lock your doors," he said. "You need to make sure that strangers can't walk into your house."

She sighed. "That may not be an issue much longer."

His heart contracted to hear the sadness and frustration in her voice. "You haven't figured out a way to keep the house?"

"No."

"Have you tried reasoning with your sister?"

She emitted a bitter laugh. "Reason with her?" she asked. "We can barely speak to each other."

He didn't have family. But if grudges and lawsuits were any indication of how family treated each other, he might not have missed much.

"I'm sorry," he said. *For so much...*

"I thought you didn't understand why the house means so much to me."

"I don't," he admitted. "But it obviously matters a lot to you, so I'm sorry."

She stared up at him now, but he doubted she could see him because tears filled her eyes. And his heart contracted even more. He didn't want to see her cry.

He had intended to commiserate with her—not upset her. But then he'd never been good at finding the right words.

"Shh," he murmured, as much to himself as to her. It was better if he didn't try to talk. To distract her from her sadness, he kissed her. First her eyelids. Then her cheeks down which her tears trailed. He kissed her lips until she moaned and kissed him back. Maybe because they were cold—or because they were hot—they shed their damp clothes quickly. Then to really distract her, he touched her—sliding his hands all over her naked body, cupping her breasts, stroking her butt...

She pushed him down onto her bed and touched him back. He was so distracted that he barely remembered to reach for a condom. He'd barely sheathed himself before she straddled his hips and guided him to her entrance. She rode him, her movements frenzied as she sought her release.

He helped her, his hands gripping her hips. He thrust up, matching her rhythm. And they came together—crying out in pleasure.

SERENA DROPPED ONTO Cody's chest, which heaved as he struggled to breathe. She panted for breath, too, but not because of what they'd just done. She had difficulty breathing because of what she'd just realized.

She had fallen in love with Cody Mallehan.

Her friends would think she was crazy. Hell, so

would Cody. He had warned her over and over that he wasn't sticking around. But he'd also told her he wasn't a good man.

And she suspected they didn't come much better than him. He was a far better man than he wanted anyone to know. That was why he would leave—he thought it would protect them if he was gone.

"You should stay," she said. "At least until you know if you got that job or not."

He would get it. She had no doubt about that. No matter what else anyone said about Cody, they all agreed he was a good firefighter.

Even Fiona and Tammy.

He just wasn't good boyfriend material.

"You don't know the arsonist is really after you," she said.

"Who else would have cut my brake line?" he asked.

She forced a smile. "An ex-girlfriend? A jealous boyfriend of a girlfriend?"

His lips curved into a slight grin. "The only guys I've pissed off flirting with their women are Wyatt and Dawson. I hope one of them didn't cut my brake line."

"I doubt that." Despite how badly they all razzed each other, it was clear they loved him, too.

"So it has to be the arsonist," he said. "And because of that, I really think I should go."

She drew back and asked him, "Are you just looking for an excuse to leave?"

"Serena, I told you—"

She pressed her fingers to his lips. "Don't worry," she said. "I know you're not the kind of guy who can stay in one place for very long. You told me all that. I don't imagine you living in this house with me—raising kids with me here."

"Is that why you want to keep it?" he asked.

She nodded. "I want to raise my family here like my grandmother and my mother did," she confirmed.

He stared at her, but his green gaze was blank. He had no reference point to compare his life to the one she wanted. He had never had a family or a home.

She could give that to him…if he wanted. But it was clear that he didn't. He couldn't miss what he'd never had. If she tried to convince him to stay, it would be too hard on him. He'd grow bored because traveling from place to place was all he knew.

"I'm sorry that I thought it was just a house," he murmured. Maybe he thought she had started crying over the house, when the cause was his sweetness, the realization that she'd fallen for him…

"To you, it's just a house," she agreed. "And that's *why* I know you're not the guy for me."

"Then what are we doing here?" he asked, as he moved inside her.

Their bodies were still joined. They were as close as two people could be, yet so far apart in how they thought and felt.

Sure, she loved him. But it didn't matter. He didn't want the same things out of life that she did.

"Why can't we stay away from each other?" he asked. "Why do I want you again after we just made love?"

"Maybe we're just a distraction for each other," she

suggested. "You're taking my mind off my sister's law-suit. And I'm..."

She waited but he said nothing, so she asked, "What am I distracting you from?"

He sighed. "Everything."

He didn't sound happy about it. But for some odd reason Serena was. He might never love her the way she loved him, but at least he wasn't indifferent to her.

And when he left, he would remember her. He wouldn't be like her father who'd left her mother without another thought.

He would think of her occasionally. But she worried that he would always be on her mind.

15

"MACK MCROONEY CALLED me again," Braden said as he joined Cody in the workout room at the firehouse. Like the other rooms, it had cement-block walls. But this room had a couple of mirrors glued over some of the blocks. "He had some questions about you."

Cody tensed, his arms straining as he held the dumbbell over his head. He studied Braden's face in one of the mirrors glued to the cement-block walls. "So did you tell him what a cocky pain in the ass I am?"

Braden sighed. "If I did that, he wouldn't want to hire you away from me."

"So does he want to?" Cody asked. He highly doubted it after the way he'd blown his interview.

Serena distracted him—from everything. But he hadn't left her. He couldn't bring himself to leave, not with a maniac on the loose.

"Sounds like he's going to offer you the position," Braden said.

Cody sucked in a breath. He'd wanted that job for so long. But now that it might be his...

"You're okay with that?" he asked his boss.

"I don't want to lose you," Braden admitted. "But I know being a smoke jumper is what you want. You made that clear when I hired you."

"And you took a chance on me anyway," Cody said. "Why? Were you just doing Mack a favor—getting me the experience he wanted?"

Braden shook his head. "Not at all. I hired you because I thought you'd fit in well with the team and that you'd work hard. And I figured that after a couple of seasons with us, you might change your mind and want to stay."

Cody wasn't so sure what he wanted anymore. "I think I should," he murmured.

Braden grinned. "Really? You'd consider staying?"

"At least until the arsonist is caught," Cody said. "I'd hate to leave now."

"We can handle him," Braden said.

Cody could have pointed out that they hadn't caught him yet. But he refrained. "This is personal to me."

"It's personal to all of us."

"But he burned down my cabin."

"He burned down the part of the forest that your cabin happened to be in," Braden said. "I'm sure he's not after you specifically."

"I'm not so certain," Cody said. "That fall I took in the tub—"

"—was an accident," Braden said.

"And my brake line getting cut?"

Braden tensed now. "What?"

Cody had intended to tell Braden when he'd gotten back from his interview. But he'd had to see Serena first to make certain she was all right. And then she'd distracted him as she always did with her sexiness, with her sweetness.

"That's how I crashed my truck," he said. "The mechanic confirmed it. He saved the brake line for us to turn in to the police."

Braden nodded. "Good. We'll call the state police and report it."

"I think we should also check out this guy staying at Serena's," he said.

Sure, Mr. Tremont was a veteran, but that didn't mean he was above committing any crimes. He gave Braden the name.

His boss nodded. He would make sure Wendell Tremont was thoroughly investigated.

"What else can we do?" Cody wondered aloud. He didn't feel like he was doing enough to keep Serena safe. Sure he'd stayed in her bed all night, his arms wrapped tightly around her. He'd been awake and alert to any sound. But the only noise he heard was Annie, pushing her way through the door to join them in bed.

"We're doing everything we can," Braden said. "I think you should take that job now."

"Why?" Cody asked. "Do you think the arsonist will leave Northern Lakes alone if I leave?"

"No," another voice chimed in as Dawson joined them. "I thought that the fires would stop when Avery left." He'd done everything in his power to make her leave—even rejecting her when he'd already fallen hopelessly in love. He hadn't lasted long, though, before he'd gone chasing after her. Actually he hadn't had to chase her; Avery had come back for him.

Cody waited for the flash of disgust and pity he'd felt for Dawson and Wyatt falling in love. But he didn't feel it. Instead he felt a little fear.

But that had to be because of the arsonist.

The fires had stopped for a little while after Avery had left and things had stayed quiet for a time even when she'd returned, between assignments, to Northern Lakes. But eventually the fires had started springing up again on the already scorched land. But the arsonist hadn't lit any fires for a few weeks. Instead he'd taken to slicking down tubs and cutting brake lines.

"You just don't want Cody to leave," Braden said.

"And you do?" Hess asked their superintendent.

Braden shrugged.

Cody began to suspect his boss might have another reason for wanting him gone: Serena. Maybe he wanted Cody out of her house so that he had a clear shot at getting her attention. He was the kind of guy she wanted—he'd appreciate her house and her heritage and her desire to raise a family where she'd grown up.

Braden was older. He'd already been ready to start his family when his wife had left him for another man.

Yeah, Braden Zimmer was the kind of guy Serena wanted and needed. But why did the thought of her with anyone but him make Cody feel sick?

SERENA FELT SICK. Maybe it was the wine. She hadn't had anything to drink since that night at the Filling Station. And this wine was too sweet.

Or maybe it was the dinner. The meat was covered in some kind of rich gravy that made her stomach feel as if it were curdling. Maybe it was the heat emanating from the candle that burned too brightly on the table between them.

But Serena suspected she felt sick because the man sitting across from her was Gordon, who smiled at her now. He was a good-looking man. He was even blond like Cody, but his hair was shorter, neater. And his eyes were blue—a clear, bright blue. He was handsome. And he was nice. But he wasn't Cody.

She wasn't on a date, though. At least it wasn't a date in her mind. She'd asked Gordon out, but she'd made it clear that she wanted to talk about what she could do in order to get a mortgage or a business loan for the boardinghouse.

Maybe she should have asked him back to the house. Maybe she should have showed him what she was trying to save. But then she would have risked running into Cody.

He hadn't been home very often over the past few days. But he still came back to the house to sleep—usually in her bed. Of course they didn't do much sleeping.

Maybe that was why she felt sick—because she was so tired. And Gordon hadn't given her anything but compliments. He had no helpful advice for her to be able to get a loan.

"The only thing you can do is talk to your sister," he suggested.

She sighed. "That's what Cody said."

"Of course," Gordon said. "I heard Cody Mallehan's been staying at your boardinghouse."

She wasn't surprised people knew; Cody was always a topic of gossip. "Yes, he is."

"Do you think that's wise?" Gordon asked as he sipped his sweet wine.

"Why wouldn't it be?" she asked.

Disapproval pulled his lips into a thin line. He didn't have Cody's kissable mouth. "I've heard he has quite the reputation."

"You know Northern Lakes," she said. "It's a small town so rumors spread. That doesn't mean they're true."

Gordon chuckled. "Rumors get started for a reason." He gestured toward the other side of the restaurant. "Like that…"

Serena glanced toward where the bank officer pointed. Cody sat at a table near the windows overlooking the street, his blond head bent toward his dinner companion. The woman's back was to Serena, so she could only see her short, dark hair.

Who was she? And what was Cody doing with her? Dating her?

But sleeping in Serena's bed every night?

The woman jumped up from the table and rushed out. Maybe she'd just learned what Serena had just discovered—that she wasn't the only woman in Cody's life.

She'd felt nausea before, but it was nothing in comparison to how she felt now. Maybe he wasn't the good guy she'd convinced herself he was. Of course, she was with another man. But it wasn't a date.

Gordon chuckled again. "Apparently everything I've

heard about Cody Mallehan isn't true," he said. "Looks like he just struck out."

It wouldn't be his last time that night. If he dared come to her bedroom again…

She glanced over to his table again, glaring at him. This time—without his dinner companion to distract him—he saw her and glared back. He was so focused on her that he must not have seen the waiter passing his table with a tray of drinks—because he lurched to his feet and bumped into the guy. The liquid flew, spraying over Cody, the waiter and the nearest diners. The glasses dropped to the hardwood floor and shattered.

The restaurant fell eerily silent as everyone stared at the debacle—at Cody. But he was still focused on her so that, as he stepped forward, he slipped on the spilled liquid and broken glass and went down with an oath that echoed throughout the restaurant.

"That's embarrassing," Gordon murmured.

But that was nothing—because Cody regained his feet with a few more curses and another fall, and staggered toward their table.

His words slurred, he demanded to know, "What the hell are you doing?"

She wondered that herself. Why had she been sleeping with a man like Cody Mallehan? A man who cared only about the conquest and not the long run?

Gordon stood. "She's on a date," he said. "Just as you must have been." He shook his head. "Although I can understand why she left."

Serena saw Cody's hand curl into a fist. Before he could swing it, she jumped up and grabbed his arm.

"You're making a scene," she told him between clenched teeth. She was so angry she felt like hitting him. She didn't care what the other diners would think, but she did want to look like a responsible business owner in front of Gordon.

"Then take me home," he said, his green eyes hard as he stared at her. Hard and intense—not glassy or bloodshot. He was furious, but she wasn't certain he was drunk despite his smelling like a brewery.

"That's rude," Gordon said. "She hasn't even finished her meal. The maître d' will call you a cab." He gestured for the waiter.

Serena grabbed her purse from the table. "That's fine," she said. "I will drive him."

"But why?" Gordon asked, and his blue eyes dimmed with disappointment.

She'd thought she'd made it clear to him that their dinner out was not a date. Driving Cody home gave her an excuse to end it now—before Gordon tried to walk her to her car, before he tried to kiss her or secure another date.

"She owes me," Cody said. "I drove her home when she drank too much at the bar."

Pitching her voice low, she said, "I don't owe you anything."

Then she forced a smile for Gordon. "I'm sorry," she said. "But I should get him home."

"He's not your responsibility," Gordon insisted.

"He's my boarder," she said. And that was all he ever should have been.

Cody slung his arm around her shoulders and leaned

heavily on her. "You better get me home before I pass out," he murmured. "You won't be able to carry me as easily as I carried you."

Her face heated as embarrassment rushed over her. She had been a mess that night at the Filling Station. But a gentleman wouldn't have mentioned it. Apparently he'd only acted like one that night.

"You're a jerk," she said, steering him quickly toward the door. She would drive him home, just in case he wasn't sober enough; then she would let him have it.

16

CODY COULD FEEL Serena's slender body bristling with anger. She was beyond pissed, and he didn't blame her.

But he was pissed, too.

"So that was good old Gordon," he murmured. His stomach knotted—like it had when he'd glanced over and seen her all dressed up sitting with another man.

"Who was *your* date?" she asked as she shoved him up against the side of her car. She pulled open the passenger's door and pushed him into the seat a little roughly.

"You didn't recognize her?"

She stared down at him. "Do I know her?"

"She used to live in Northern Lakes," he said.

Serena must not have cared that much because she didn't ask him any more questions. She just slammed the passenger's door and headed around the front of the car to the driver's side. When she moved to jam the keys in the ignition, he caught her hand.

"She wasn't my date," he qualified.

"Looked like a date."

"It definitely was *not*," he said. And there were several reasons that it hadn't been, Serena being the biggest one. But he was too proud to admit that. "I don't go out with anyone during wildfire season."

"Then what are *we* doing?" she asked.

He wondered that, too. "We're just distracting each other, remember?"

She uttered a ragged sigh.

"You're certainly distracting me." He needed to be focused on finding the arsonist; instead he was trying to help her. That hadn't turned out all that well, though. Instead he'd embarrassed her.

Not that he was actually drunk. He'd only acted that way to get her to drive him home. While he hadn't had any alcohol, he smelled like it thanks to his collision with the waiter. When he'd seen Serena with another man, he'd been so furious that he'd wanted to tear the guy apart. So he'd jumped up without realizing how horrible his timing had been.

"I'm sorry," he said. "I shouldn't have interrupted your dinner." He was always telling Serena that he was leaving soon; he shouldn't have been surprised that she would move on with someone more suitable.

He let go of her hand and sat back in his seat. He didn't think she would be able to keep her house, though. He'd tried, but he hadn't been any more successful at helping her than he'd been at catching the arsonist.

She turned the key and started the car. But she turned toward him before backing out and said, "I wasn't on a date either."

Feeling a little lighter, his heart lifted. "That's not what Gordon thinks."

"I should have made myself clearer with him," she said. "I only asked to meet with him to discuss how I might get a loan with his bank."

"Gordon's the loan officer?" The one who'd already turned her down. Now he wished he'd hit him. Not that he would have. He only stepped in to stop bar brawls; he never started them, although he'd been tempted to tonight.

"Yes…" She sighed again. "It was a waste of time. His only suggestion was to talk to my sister." She drove for a few miles in silence before adding, "You're not going to say 'I told you so'?"

"Why would I do that?"

"Because you suggested the same thing."

But now he knew that talking to her sister wouldn't help; it wouldn't change Courtney's mind. And it would probably only cause Serena more frustration and pain.

"I was wrong," he said. "So's Gordon."

She peered across the console at him. "That wasn't…" She shook her head. "Of course it wasn't. Courtney would never come back to Northern Lakes."

Despite being her twin, Serena really didn't know her sister well. But Cody couldn't correct her—not without inciting her anger. She would be furious if she knew what he'd done—that he'd probably just made everything worse.

He couldn't help her, but maybe he could distract her from her worries. He reached across the console and closed his hand over her bare knee.

"I can understand why Gordon would be confused," he said. "You're dressed like you were on a date."

She wore some kind of gauzy sundress that tied over her bare shoulders. It was the color of sunshine and made her tanned skin look even more golden. His fingers itched to untie those little straps and lower her top so he could feast on her breasts.

The skirt was short, leaving her long legs tantalizingly bare. It rode up when she sat down. So his hand rode up, too, skimming up the inside of her smooth thigh.

She squirmed in the seat. "Unless you want me to hit a tree, you better stop that," she warned him.

Her skin was so silky and warm. And the farther up his hand traveled, the softer and warmer she was.

"It might be worth it," he murmured, as he touched the lacy edge of her panties. He could slide his fingers under, could stroke the very core of her...

"I'm not sure you could handle another knock on the head."

He wasn't sure he could either. But he hadn't been thinking clearly even before he'd gotten the concussion. He asked, "Do you mean from hitting the tree or from you hitting me?"

In the glow of the dash lights, her lips curved into a slight smile. "I *should* hit you in the head."

"You should," he agreed. Maybe she could knock some sense into him.

"I almost did," she said. "I almost hit you..."

"I wouldn't have blamed you," he said. "I embarrassed you." He moved his fingertip along the lacy edge of her panties. "You should really let me make that up to you…"

She jerked the wheel, and one of the car's tires dropped into the gravel on the soft shoulder.

Cody pulled his hand out from beneath her skirt and grabbed the dash.

But she laughed and easily steered back onto the road. "Don't worry. I have control of my car."

SERENA GOT THEM safely home, but she never regained control of Cody. Despite her threats, he hadn't stopped touching her. Heat and moisture pooled between her legs, where her body throbbed with desire for him.

As she stepped out of the car, her legs wobbled. He had literally made her weak in the knees. And in will-power. She should have been furious with him. He had embarrassed her. And he didn't even have the excuse of being drunk. She wondered if he'd had anything to drink at all.

Maybe the woman he'd been with had been the person interviewing him for the smoke jumper position. Serena shouldn't have just assumed the boss would be a man. Women were Hotshots, too. There were two on his team.

But the woman hadn't looked happy when she'd left. She hadn't shaken his hand or patted his arm or done anything encouraging. Maybe he hadn't gotten the job. But that didn't mean he still wouldn't leave.

Serena had no doubt that he would. He wasn't staying in Northern Lakes. So, when he met her at the front of the car and tried to wrap his arms around her, she dodged him and headed for the stairs.

But he caught up with her on the porch. Looping an arm around her waist, he drew her back against his chest. His lips slid along her neck, and he whispered in her ear, "Let's go to bed…"

"You're drunk," she said, although she knew he'd only been faking. She pulled away from him and stepped inside the house. Lights glowed within; the house was always so warm—so welcoming. Sadness tugged at her as she wondered if the house would feel the same for another owner. But she couldn't think about that now—not without tears threatening.

She focused on Cody instead. He was so good at taking her mind off her worries. He reached for her again, dragging her body up against the long, hard length of his.

"That's why you have to put me to bed," he told her, his mouth nibbling at the corners of hers. "I can't take care of myself right now."

She laughed at his outrageousness. She'd never known anyone more self-reliant. But she pretended to help him up the first flight of stairs. He wasn't leaning on her, though. When he moved to ascend the next flight—to her quarters—she pulled him to a stop.

"You must be in bad shape," she said, clicking her tongue against her teeth in mock-pity. "You've forgotten that your room is on this floor."

"That's probably because I don't spend much time there," he said, and his green eyes glittered with desire. "I sleep better with you."

Or they didn't sleep at all. She shook her head. "I can't take advantage of you."

He chuckled. "Are you too much of a gentlewoman?"

"Yes," she said.

He swung her up in his arms and carried her that last flight of stairs. As he pushed open the door, he told her, "I'm not drunk."

She sighed regretfully. "I know," she said. "But I wish you were."

"Why?"

"So you would make a fool of yourself like I did that night," she said. Or at least she thought she had. She didn't remember everything she'd done.

"You just talked a lot," he said.

That had been the next morning, though, after making love with him. That was when she'd told him about the lawsuit.

He grinned. "I've been told I already talk too much."

She'd heard Wyatt and Dawson say so. But that had been because he'd been needling them about Fiona and Avery.

"You don't talk about yourself, though," she said.

His grin slipped away, leaving his handsome face looking more serious than she'd ever seen it—except for that day he'd crashed into the tree. "I've told you more about myself than I've ever told anyone else."

She believed him. "I know."

"You know me better than anyone else."

Unfortunately she did.

She sighed and nodded.

"So you know it wouldn't matter how drunk I was,"

he warned her. "I'm never going to be able to say what you want to hear."

That he would never leave...

That he loved her.

All she really wanted—even more than her house—was him. And just like the house, she had no way of hanging on to him.

He would never truly be hers.

17

CODY HATED HIMSELF for putting that look on her face—the one of disappointment and sadness. If only he could have given her good news about her house tonight…

But he'd messed up that, too.

Although he couldn't make her happy—in the happily-ever-after way—he could give her pleasure for a little while. He closed his arms around her and pulled her close. Burying his face in her silky hair, he sighed and murmured, "You smell like booze."

She giggled. "That's from you leaning all over me. You reek."

He swung her up in his arms and headed toward the bathroom. "Then we better shower."

"I'm not sure it's safe to shower with you," she mused as he set her on her feet in the bathroom. It had been built into a dormer, so the ceiling was high enough that he could stand up straight. The room was all octagonal marble tiles—the floor and the walls. He turned on the shower and, fully clothed, stepped under the spray.

"You're crazy!" Serena told him.

So he pulled her under the water with him. She

squealed in protest as the water saturated her dress and hair. But she was laughing, too.

He loved seeing her happy. It wouldn't last, but he refused to think about that at the moment. He reached for one of those ties on her shoulders. It was straining as the fabric grew heavy, the already loose knot stretching. The material dipped, revealing the cups of her strapless bra.

He tugged on the tie until it unknotted. Then he undid the other knot as well. The wet, sunny-yellow material dropped to the floor. The water was warm but goose bumps lifted on her tanned skin. He wanted her hot—not cold. So he removed her bra and lowered his mouth to her breast. Her nipple had already tightened into a bud. He plucked at it with his lips, then swept the tip of his tongue across it.

She moaned and tangled her fingers in his wet hair. "Cody…"

He pushed her wet panties down her legs until they dropped onto the dress and bra. Then he moved his fingers between her thighs. She shifted her legs and leaned against him. She needed him like he needed her; she needed the release—the pleasure.

His body ached and throbbed with tension. Then her hands were there, freeing him from his pants. Her wet fingers stroked him to madness. But he fought for control. He couldn't take pleasure until he'd given it—until he'd made her as crazy as she made him.

He dropped to his knees, the water swirling over his head and shoulders. And he lifted her, so that her legs straddled his shoulders. He buried his face between her legs. His hands kneaded her sweet ass as he clutched her closer. She arched against him—needing more.

He closed his lips over her clit and gently sucked on it. Then he teased it with the tip of his tongue as he moved his fingers inside her, stroking. After a few minutes she clenched tight around his fingers.

"Cody!" His name was a cry of shock and pleasure.

She drove him crazy with her sweetness. He needed her—needed to bury himself deeply in her wetness, her heat. He slid her legs down his shoulders as he stood up. Her legs locked around his waist, and he eased his cock into her.

Home. This was home. Not a house that was over a century old. Her body—that felt like where he belonged for the first time. Overwhelmed with sensations, he came quickly.

What had she done to him? How had Serena Beaumont made him feel things he had never felt before?

It wasn't fair—not when he'd already failed her.

"I'm sorry," he murmured.

She deserved to realize all the dreams she'd dreamed. But just as he hadn't been able to think of a way to stop the arsonist, he hadn't been able to think of a way to save her house for her.

SERENA BIT HER LIP to hold back the declaration. She wanted to tell Cody she loved him. But that wouldn't be fair. He had already apologized because he knew he couldn't give her what she wanted.

He needed to move on. It was the pattern of his life—one so ingrained she doubted he could change even if he wanted to. And he clearly didn't. He wanted the job in Washington, which offered more adventure. More danger...

She couldn't stop him from chasing his dream. He would only come to resent her for it—like her sister resented Serena. Courtney could have been the woman he'd met with in the restaurant. It had been years since Serena had seen her. But why would he have bothered to contact Courtney when he didn't understand her dreams any more than she understood his?

They made love again that night—but it was bittersweet. When she awoke a few hours later, she was alone. The bed was still warm; Cody hadn't been gone long.

Would he be back?

Or had last night been his way of saying goodbye?

Tears stung her eyes and her nose. When she sniffled, she smelled it: the smoke. There was a fire. Her heart pounding furiously with fear, she jumped out of bed and pulled open drawers, grabbing clothes. She dressed so quickly she managed to button her jean shorts before the smoke alarms blared.

The fire must have just started. Hopefully there would be time to get everyone out of the house.

"Fire!" she yelled as she passed the second floor. Stanley and Mr. Tremont were young enough to get themselves out of the house. She was more worried about Mrs. Gulliver and Mr. Stehouwer. They slept without their hearing aids, so they probably wouldn't even notice the alarms were blaring.

What about Cody? Where was he?

He caught her at the bottom of the stairs, his arms sliding around her. "It's okay," he said. "The fire's out."

Of course he would have smelled the smoke first. He was probably conditioned to.

Trembling, she clutched at him. "Is everyone all right?"

"Yes," he assured her. "It was nothing. Just a little smoke really." But a muscle twitched in his cheek, and he had that look on his face again—the one that had chilled her when he'd crashed his truck into the tree.

"Someone set it," she surmised. And she shivered as she realized the arsonist had been in her home again.

His broad shoulders—bare like his chest—lifted in a slight shrug. "I don't know for certain. Could have just been a cigarette dropped outside."

"It wasn't in the house?" she asked hopefully.

He shook his head.

"But the fire alarms went off."

"All the windows were open, and the smoke blew inside, setting off the detectors."

She expelled a shaky breath. "So it was probably nothing."

But he didn't look like he thought it was nothing. He looked mad. And when the door creaked open in the foyer, he let her go and ran toward the noise.

Serena ran after him; she didn't care if it was dangerous. She wanted to make sure Cody was safe—even more than she wanted to protect her other boarders.

An oath rang out. And a fist flew. Something fell over. She could see only shadows grappling in the darkness—

pounding on each other. She flipped on the lights and yelled, "Stop!"

Cody paused midswing and stared down at the person lying under him on the foyer floor. "What the hell are you doing creeping around in the middle of the night?"

Mr. Tremont stared up at him through an eye already beginning to swell. Then the other man turned toward her. "I didn't realize there was a curfew and consequences for breaking it."

She might get sued yet. "Cody, let him up!"

Why had he fought with another boarder? She would have understood if Mr. Tremont had been an intruder. But he had every reason for being in the house, too. He paid to live there.

Cody shook his head. "I want to know what the hell he's doing sneaking around like he always does."

"I was out," Tremont replied.

And something about his tone—an evasiveness to it—chilled Serena. Why did he never say where he was going or what he was doing or when he'd be back?

Stanley always told her, and he was a teenager. He was the one who was supposed to be slinking secretively around—not a grown man.

Serena, who had made a point of always honoring her boarders' privacy, asked him, "Where were you?"

The gray-haired man turned to her in surprise—probably at her suspiciousness.

"Were you setting a fire in the backyard?" Cody asked him.

"That's ridiculous," Tremont replied. "Just like having to check in with my landlady. But if you must know, I just got back from having dinner and drinks in town." He shoved at Cody. "Now let me up so I can go to bed."

A gnarled hand wrapped around Serena's arm. "Must be nice, dear, having two young men fight over you." Mrs. Gulliver gazed wistfully at them—especially at the shirtless Cody. "I can still remember what that was like…"

Serena could imagine that she had had plenty of suitors brawling over her. Even at eighty-six, with her pink-and-purple hair, the woman was a stunner.

"They're not fighting over me, Mrs. Gulliver," she said loudly, since there were no aides in the elderly woman's ears. She wasn't certain why they'd been fighting once they'd identified each other, though. But Cody was still edgy.

Because of the arsonist…

With a polite nod at Serena and Mrs. Gulliver and no glance for Cody at all, Mr. Tremont got to his feet and headed up the front stairwell. She would need to talk to him in the morning—apologize and explain.

But if she told him about the mishaps that had happened around the house, he might move. Would it matter, though, when she was probably going to lose the house anyway?

"There was a fire in the backyard, Mrs. G," Cody said. "I was trying to find out who started it."

The old woman snorted. "That stupid Mr. Stehouwer must have been sneaking smokes again. I've told him that he needs to make certain they're out or he's going to burn the whole house down." She patted Serena's arm. "Of course we would never let that happen, though."

"No," Cody said. "We certainly wouldn't."

We?

The word echoed mockingly inside Serena's mind.

How could he say that when he had no intention of sticking around? He shouldn't be making the older woman or Serena any promises that he wouldn't be around to keep. He had warned her that he would break her heart. He might have been joking at the time, but that was one promise he could have made.

Serena was certain that one would come true.

18

CODY WAS FURIOUS with himself but mostly with Serena. She had no right to make him feel so much. On some level he had known moving into the boardinghouse was going to be a mistake. That was why he'd crashed at the firehouse as long as he had. But even he hadn't realized how big a mistake it would be.

He'd had no idea that it was going to hurt this damn bad when he had to leave her.

Cody had punished his body with weights until sweat dripped off him onto the concrete floor of the workout room. But the physical exertion had given him no relief from the emotions gripping him. It hadn't eased any of the pressure in his chest as he thought of what he had to do.

"What the hell's wrong with you?" Braden asked him. "You look like you kicked your own ass in here."

Cody pushed his sweat-slick hair back from his face and focused on his boss. "You're the one who tells us to do daily workouts," he reminded him.

"That was more than a workout," Braden said as he dropped onto the bench next to him. "Are you worried you're not getting the smoke jumper job? I told you it sounded like Mack really wants you."

Cody's hand shook slightly as he picked up his cell phone from the bench and slid it back into his pocket. Just a short while ago he had taken the call—the official offer for the position. He needed to tell Braden that he'd accepted it. But he felt like he owed it to Serena to tell her first. Not that she would be surprised.

He was. He hadn't really believed he would get it— maybe because he'd wanted it so much and for so long. Just like—as a kid—he had wanted a family of his own. But he'd never gotten one of those. He'd learned to expect nothing out of life and avoid disappointment that way.

"I've got to tell you something," he told his boss. Maybe he was just stalling now—buying himself some time before he talked to Serena.

Braden tilted his head. "You sound serious for once. What's it about?"

"The guy," Cody said, "the one living at the boardinghouse…"

Braden tensed. "Wendell Tremont. You think he's the arsonist?"

Cody almost wished he was; then he wouldn't feel bad about beating him up a few nights ago. No, given what he'd learned, he didn't feel bad. Well, not for anyone but Braden. "He's not the arsonist."

"Are you absolutely sure?" Braden asked. "I've started checking him out. Tremont has been in town for a while. He showed up around the time that first fire started. It could be him."

"He's here because of you," Cody told him.

"What?"

He hadn't been able to pound the truth out of the guy. He'd shared a bottle of whiskey with Tremont and apologized for beating on him. Serena wasn't the only one who talked too much when she'd been drinking.

"Your ex's new husband doesn't trust her any more than you should have," he shared. "Tremont is a private detective hired to watch you—to make sure Amy hasn't been sneaking around with you behind her husband's back."

He had expected Braden to be upset—either sad or outraged. He was surprised when the superintendent laughed instead. "That's hilariously ironic."

"Yes, it is," Cody agreed. Then he laughed, too.

"The guy she cheated on me with now thinks she's cheating on him with me." Braden laughed harder. Maybe a little too hard.

But maybe this was what the superintendent needed to finally be able to move on.

Would Serena miss Cody like Braden had his wife?

"Go home and pack," his boss told him.

Did he know that Cody had already accepted the position? Cody had told Mack McRooney he needed to work out his notice first. He'd thought the other man would have respected that. "W-why—" he stammered the question "—do you want me to pack?"

"We've been called up to relieve a team on the California fires." He narrowed his eyes and studied Cody's face. "I mentioned at the last meeting that we were going next time we got called up."

Cody nodded. "Of course. I remember."

But it felt like so much had happened since that meeting.

"I thought you'd be happy," Braden said.

"I am." This was good. He needed this last trip out with the team. But first he had to tell Serena goodbye.

SERENA FOUND HIM PACKING. This wasn't throwing-just-a-few-things-in-a-duffel-bag packing. This was making-sure-he-had-everything-he-owned packing. Nothing was left on the table beside the bed, which he had also made up despite hardly ever having used it.

This was saying-goodbye packing.

But he hadn't sought her out to say anything. He had slipped quietly into the house. Maybe he'd hoped to leave without telling her—like he had the day he'd crashed his truck into the tree.

"Where are you going?" she asked, surprised she could hear her voice over the sound of her pounding heart.

"California," he replied without glancing up. He must have heard her walk into the room, but he had yet to really acknowledge her presence.

"I thought that the smoke jumper position was in Washington," she said.

"It is." He wouldn't look at her. Instead he seemed focused on the clothes he was folding into the duffel bag lying on top of the red-and-navy blue bedspread. "I'll be going there right after we leave California."

Her heart stopped beating entirely for a moment—probably when it broke. "You got the job?"

He nodded.

She put aside her feelings and studied him. "Why aren't you happy?"

"I am," he said quickly—almost defensively.

He didn't look happy. His handsome face was tense, grim even. There was no smile on his lips. No brightness in his green eyes. If he was happy, she might have been able to forgive him for leaving.

She would have been happy had she been able to figure out a way to keep her house—because that was what she truly wanted. This position wasn't what Cody truly wanted. She realized that now.

"You don't want this job," she accused him.

"I applied for it two years ago," he told her. "I wanted to be a smoke jumper more than I've wanted to be a Hotshot. Being a Hotshot was my only way to get the experience I needed."

She focused on only the first part of what he'd told her. "That was two years ago," she said. "So you don't want it anymore."

He shook his head—almost as if he was disappointed in her. "You don't know what I want."

But she did. "I know you better than anyone else ever has," she said. "You told me that yourself."

"Serena…"

"So I know what you're doing," she said. "You're running!"

He smiled now, but it was really just a faint curving of his lips. "I'm working," he said. "That's what I do."

A twinge struck her heart, and Serena sucked in a breath at the pain. Her heart was definitely breaking.

Was this how her mother had felt when her father had abandoned her and their unborn children? Her father had been a coward; she saw now that Cody was, too.

"Run," she told him. "That's all you're doing. You don't care about that job anymore. You're just scared that you care too much about your team and the people here in Northern Lakes. About me…"

His green eyes narrowed and grew hard with anger. "I have been honest with you from the very beginning," he said.

She couldn't deny that.

"I warned you that I'm not the man you're looking for."

"I should have listened to you," she admitted. "I wish I had." Fervently. Then she wouldn't know what she was losing when he left.

"You'll find that guy you really want," he said. "Maybe you already have. Maybe it's Gordon or Braden…"

He definitely didn't love her if he could talk so casually of passing her off to another man. Why had she thought she loved him? Because how could love be real if it wasn't reciprocated?

He ran his hand over his face, as if trying to block out the sight of her. "I'm sorry, Serena."

She was, too—so sorry.

"I've gotta go—"

"—to California," she said. "Then Washington. Will you ever come back to Northern Lakes?"

He shook his head. "No."

She blinked back the tears stinging her eyes. "I

thought I knew you," she said. "I thought I understood you."

"You're a jerk!" The words hadn't come from her mouth. It was Stanley who hurled them through the door Serena had left open. "I can't believe you're just taking off! Were you even going to say goodbye to me?"

Cody's face flushed, and she wondered if he had planned to or if he'd just intended to slip out unnoticed. Maybe he really was a coward.

"Of course I was going to say goodbye," he insisted.

Stanley's breath escaped in a gasp—like Cody had punched him. "So it's really goodbye then? You're not coming back to Northern Lakes?"

Serena had been wrong about Cody. But these two shared a bond—growing up in foster homes—that she couldn't fathom.

"I got the job in North Cascades," Cody said.

Stanley's voice quavered as he said, "The smoke jumper job…"

Cody nodded.

The kid's eyes and nose grew red. His heart was breaking, too. Serena saw it in his face. Then he turned and ran from the room.

She moved to run after him, but Cody caught her arm, holding on to her. "Let me go!" she yelled. But even as she said it, she knew she was the one who had to let go.

19

CODY HATED THE FEELINGS of pain and regret coursing through him. He wanted to run after Serena and Stanley. He wanted to hurl his duffel bag out the window and tell them he wasn't leaving. But even if he turned down the smoke jumper position, he couldn't stay—not indefinitely. It wasn't in his nature. They should know that, too.

He had already stayed too long if they'd begun to doubt that, if they'd begun to think differently. He shouldn't have given them a false impression of him.

He stared out of his window into the backyard where Stanley kicked the pile of dirt Cody had used to put out the fire the other night. The cigarette had set a dead shrub on fire. Had it really been Mr. Stehouwer's?

The eighty-seven-year-old didn't remember going outside to smoke that night. But he was sometimes confused. And they had found a pack of cigarettes in his room—the same brand that had started the fire. It must have been an accident. The arsonist would have been bolder about his actions.

But then slicking down a bathtub and cutting a brake

line hadn't been especially bold. They'd been the sneaky actions of a coward.

He could tell Serena thought he was one. She had accused him of running. But she was wrong.

He'd wanted the more solitary life of a smoke jumper. While their teams could be as big as the Hotshots, they usually weren't. He could parachute in with a small crew—just a couple other jumpers. Or he might get sent in alone.

That was good, though. That was the way he'd wanted it. No responsibility to anyone but himself. That way he couldn't let down anyone—like Serena. And Stanley.

No. He had no reason to run.

SERENA REACHED OUT for Stanley, but the kid spun away from her as if he couldn't stand to be touched. She had noticed that about him before—how he shied away from physical contact. Had he been abused?

Was that part of why Cody had been so protective of him? But he wasn't protective enough to stick around to make sure no one else hurt the kid. No, he'd hurt him himself.

"Are you okay?" she asked the teenager.

He nodded, tousling his mop of already messy curls. "I'm okay." He scrubbed his hands over his face, wiping away every trace of the tears he'd been crying when she'd found him. "Sorry I'm acting like such a baby."

"You're not." She felt like crying, too. "I understand why you're upset."

He snorted derisively. "Because I'm a selfish jerk?"

"You're not," she said. And she reached for him again. He let her hand rest on his shoulder, let her squeeze it in reassurance.

"Yes, I am," he insisted miserably. "It's selfish to be mad. I should be happy for Cody. I should be congratulating him. It's a huge deal to get the smoke jumper job. He wanted it even before he got kicked out of his last foster home, where we lived together. He had posters hanging up on his wall. I can still remember him rolling them up when he had to pack up and leave."

She'd thought her heart was breaking before. She had had no idea. She'd also had no idea just how long Cody had wanted the job. She'd thought it was just for a couple of years. But it had been longer than that.

"But instead of being happy for him," Stanley said, "all I can be is sad for myself—because I'm going to miss him." He uttered a ragged sigh. "That's selfish."

Put that way it sounded incredibly selfish. But she had behaved worse than Stanley had. "I understand why you feel the way you do," she said. "And it's okay to be upset because you're going to miss someone."

He shook his head again. "You grew up here—in this great house," he said. "So you don't get it. You don't know what it's like leaving a foster house. It's a good thing when someone leaves—it means they finally got a home."

"But that's not the case here," she said. Cody was leaving his home.

"Getting that job," Stanley said, "that's like getting adopted to Cody. It's like he's finally getting his family."

And she'd wanted to take that from him. She glanced

up at the window of his room. But he wasn't standing there. She could have sworn that she'd felt his gaze on them. But there wasn't so much as a shadow moving about the room.

Maybe he had already left.

Since the crash, he'd been using one of the US Forest Service trucks, though, and she would have heard it pull out of the driveway if he'd driven off.

"Too bad we don't have time to throw him a party," Stanley said.

"Party?" a deep voice repeated. "You want to celebrate my leaving?"

"He wants to congratulate you," Serena said, bracing herself to turn to Cody.

"Yeah," Stanley said. "Sorry I was such a stupid jerk. I know this is what you want—that you're really happy."

But Cody didn't look happy. He looked tense and sad—like she felt. Had she done that to him? Had she stolen his happiness with her selfishness?

She drew in a deep breath and said, "Congratulations." But her voice quavered on the word. She fought back the tears threatening to overwhelm her. She had to be strong like Stanley.

She couldn't hold Cody back from his dream.

"Yeah, congratulations," Stanley said. And he grabbed Cody, wrapping his arms tightly around him. He held him for a long moment.

"I'll be in touch," Cody promised the kid, and for just a second he leaned his face against Stanley's curls before pulling away. "I'll make sure you're taking care of Annie and attending all of your classes."

Stanley nodded. "I will. I promise."

It hurt too much to watch them say goodbye. So Serena hurried away—back into her office. But she hadn't been inside long when she heard heavy boots hitting the steps of the porch. She'd just brushed away some tears when a dark shadow filled the small parlor.

"You ran away before I could give you this," he said, and he put a check on her desk.

She blinked back more tears to focus on it. Ironic that she'd run away when that was what she had accused him of doing. Apparently she wasn't just selfish; she was a hypocrite, too. "What's this?" she asked, as she read the numbers on the check. "If it's for Stanley's rent, it's way too much. I can't take all of this. I have to put the house up for sale. It could sell quickly."

"I doubt that," he murmured. "I'm not sure who else would want to take care of a place this size."

She flinched. But she couldn't argue with him. It was a lot of work.

"Even if I don't sell it right away, that's still too much money for Stanley's rent." She tried to hand back the check.

But Cody shoved his hands into his pockets. "I tried to give it to your sister the other night. She wouldn't take it from me."

"What?" Emotion squeezed her already hurting heart. "So that was Courtney the other night—in the restaurant?" Here in Northern Lakes.

He nodded. "I did an online search and contacted her through a fashion blog she started," he explained.

"But how did you get her to meet you?"

He shrugged. But she suspected she knew; Cody could be damn charming. "I told her I'd get her the money she wants."

"That figures…" Serena had been hurt before, but now she was even more disappointed about her sister's lawsuit.

He shook his head. "She wouldn't take the check no matter how hard I tried to talk her into taking it."

That was the reason their exchange had looked so intense. They had been arguing. Cody had fought for Serena.

Tears stung her eyes, but she blinked them back. "But I thought you didn't understand why I want to keep the house so badly."

"I don't," he said. "It's just a house, Serena. You're accusing me of taking this job just to run. I think you want to keep this house just to hide."

"What?"

"You feel safe here," he said. "Because it's all you know. You're afraid to try anything new—to venture out."

"Is that what Courtney told you?" she asked. Her twin had been the one who'd always urged her to try new things, to visit new places. She hadn't understood how homesick Serena got—how much she missed Mama and the house. "Is that why she wouldn't take the check?"

He shook his head. "She wouldn't take it because she doesn't want the money."

"Then why sue me?"

"To get you to sell the house," he said. "She blames

it for killing your mother. She thinks if you stay here it'll kill you, too."

She sucked in a breath. She hadn't considered how Courtney might feel—that she might see how hard their mother had worked to keep the house as the reason for the heart attack that had taken her life.

Serena shook her head. "That's not true. My mother loved this house. That's why she fought to keep it. That's why I need to fight, too."

"Then use that check to get a lawyer," he suggested. "Maybe you can stop her."

"Why would you help me?" she asked. Especially after how she'd treated him.

"Because I'm not going to tell you how to live your life," he said. "If you think this house is all you need to be happy, then I want you to keep it."

But she knew that even if she could stop Courtney from forcing her to sell, she wouldn't be happy—not with Cody gone.

20

CODY COULDN'T GET the image out of his mind that he had seen out the window of his room at the boarding-house. Serena had been so sweet with Stanley, so loving and patient with the skittish teenager. She would make a great mom. A great foster mom.

Hell, her house—that outrageously big house—would be perfect to foster kids. Maybe if she switched the boardinghouse to a foster home, she could get the financing she needed to pay off her stubborn sister and satisfy the lawsuit. Courtney couldn't force her to sell if Serena could come up with the money another way. Her twin didn't know Serena at all; she had no idea how strong her twin was. Taking care of that house and everyone in it was what Serena thrived doing. Keeping it wouldn't destroy her.

Losing it might.

He stopped the truck outside the firehouse and grabbed his duffel bag off the passenger's seat. He'd no more than stepped inside before Braden was in his face. "What the hell do you think you're doing?"

He lifted the duffel bag. "What you told me to do,"

he said. "Getting ready to leave for California." But as he said it, his nerves prickled, lifting the hair on the nape of his neck.

He had a bad feeling about leaving.

"I'm not talking about that," Braden said. "I'm talking about that position in North Cascades. First you accept the job, and then you call Mack McRooney back and tell him that you don't want it?"

Cody had done that before he'd come down to Serena's office—as he'd watched Serena and Stanley from his bedroom window. "Yeah."

"I assured him that you're not flighty," Braden said. "I explained that you think you have to stay with us until the arsonist is caught."

But that was only part of it. He realized that now. Before he could explain himself, other guys started walking into the firehouse. Wyatt and Dawson hurried with their gear.

"The plane's ready," Dawson said. "We've got to get going. They think the wildfire's shifting. They need all the help they can get."

But that eerie sense of foreboding increased and Cody said, "I don't think we should go."

"What the hell's wrong with you?" Wyatt asked. "You're the one who's always raring to leave."

"When we're gone, we're leaving Northern Lakes unprotected against the arsonist for at least a couple of weeks."

"When we're gone, nothing happens here," Braden reminded him.

He didn't feel reassured, though.

"You said yourself that you think the arsonist has singled you out now," Braden persisted. "So if you're gone…"

Cody agreed, "Northern Lakes—" *and Serena* "—will be safer." He grabbed his duffel bag and followed the rest of his team out.

When he got back, he would tell Serena about his idea for how she could save her house—and a lot of kids like him and Stanley. Maybe he'd also tell her how he felt about her…if he could find the courage to admit it to himself.

Because she was right. When he'd accepted that smoke jumper job, he had been running. He'd been rejecting her before she could reject him. He'd been convinced that she would because he wasn't the kind of guy she wanted.

But what if he could be that guy for her? If he could prove it to her, she might give him a chance. She wasn't like the adoptive parents who'd returned him after a few years or the foster families who'd never let him stay.

She was loving and loyal. She wouldn't reject him. She might even love him—if he let her.

If he had that chance…

The closer they got to the fire, the more dire the situation looked. They didn't have to worry about the arsonist getting them now. They had to worry about surviving their current assignment.

"You are in Northern Lakes," Serena said as she joined her sister at her mother's graveside. There were fresh flowers lying near the granite marker; Courtney must have brought them, because Serena hadn't been able to visit for a while.

She'd been too busy trying to save the house. And too embarrassed that she'd lost her heart to the kind of man Mama had always warned her to stay away from.

"Didn't you see me the other night at the restaurant?" Courtney asked.

"I didn't recognize you," she admitted. Despite being twins, they didn't look much alike beyond their coloring. Courtney's black hair was short and stylish—like her clothes. With her skinny jeans and cropped top, she looked like she'd stepped out of a fashion magazine whereas Serena looked like she'd just stepped out of the kitchen, which was true.

If Courtney had seen her, why hadn't she said anything? Because she was embarrassed over suing? Or maybe she'd been afraid Serena would be so angry about it she'd make a scene?

"It's been a long time," Serena said. Shortly after high school graduation, Courtney had left for college and never returned. Until now.

Courtney expelled a shaky little sigh. "Yes…"

"I thought you were never coming home."

"It's not home to me," Courtney said.

"It's where we grew up—where our ancestors come from," Serena said. "It's home."

"Guess that's just one more thing we'll have to agree to disagree about," Courtney said.

"Will you sue me over that, too?"

Courtney shook her head, and her hair skimmed

across her cheek. With her more delicate features, she looked more like Mama than Serena did.

Pain clenched Serena's heart. She felt like she'd lost them both.

Courtney murmured, "I shouldn't have come back."

"Why did you?" Serena asked. "Why come back now and not for Mama's funeral?"

"It would have been too hard then," Courtney said. "Too soon. I thought I could handle it now." But tears trailed down beneath the lenses of her dark sunglasses.

Instinctively Serena reached out and clasped her twin's trembling hand. "I understand." And she did understand Courtney not being able to say goodbye to Mama.

"I *don't* understand you," Courtney said.

"I promised Mama and Grandma I would keep the house."

Courtney sighed. "They shouldn't have asked you to. It was selfish of them to decide what you had to do with your life."

Serena shook her head. "I consider it an honor."

"It's a death sentence," Courtney muttered as she gazed down at the grave.

"I don't blame it for killing Mama like you do."

"Cody told you what I said?"

She nodded. "He told me what you think—that you're worried about me." And because of that, Serena could forgive her for suing. Courtney wasn't doing it for the money; she was doing it because she thought she was helping Serena.

"The house is too much work," Courtney said. "It

was too much for Mama and for Grandma, and it's too much for you, too."

She couldn't argue with that. But that was why Serena needed someone who would stay beside her and work with her. But Cody wasn't that man.

He was already gone. The whole team was. But unlike Cody, the rest of them would come back. Fiona anxiously awaited the return of her fiancé.

"I've handled the house for a year on my own," she reminded herself more than Courtney.

"The guy who tried to buy me off—he hasn't helped?"

Serena shook her head. "He's already left. Like our father." Fortunately she hadn't gotten pregnant like Mama had.

"I found him," Courtney said.

"Cody?" She'd thought he'd sought out her twin— not the other way around.

"I found our father."

Serena gasped in surprise. "You did? Why would you bother? He abandoned our mother and us."

Courtney shook her head. "No. He abandoned Northern Lakes. He hated it here. He asked Mama to leave with him, but she refused. And she never told him about us."

"You believe him?" Serena was skeptical. It was easy for him to make these claims now, when no one was alive to contradict him.

"Yes," Courtney said. "I found him the summer after our freshman year of college. When he told me, I asked

Mama and she confirmed that everything he said was true."

"I thought she loved him so much."

"But why didn't she leave with him?" Courtney asked.

Serena knew. "Because she was afraid."

To leave Northern Lakes, to try something new.

"Is that why Cody's gone and you're still here?" Courtney asked her.

Tears stung Serena's eyes, but she blinked them back—too proud to cry any more tears over Cody Mallehan. "Because he didn't ask."

Courtney laughed, but it was a bitter, humorless sound. "He and I agree about you and that house—the only way you're going to leave it is in a pine box, just like Mama, and Grandma before her."

Serena shivered. No. She wasn't like her mother. She would leave it for love. If she believed Cody loved her...

She doubted he did, though.

But if he didn't love her, why would he have given her that check? Why would he have wanted her dreams to come true even though he hadn't understood them? He had to love her. She couldn't love him as much as she did if that love wasn't reciprocated.

But he was gone now—not just to that fire out west but to the smoke jumper job after it. She would have to wait until his Hotshot team returned to see how she could get a message to him—how she could tell him how much she loved him.

She loved him enough to leave her home and Northern Lakes—no matter how frightened that made her.

But she wasn't just frightened about leaving; she was more frightened that she might not get the opportunity. Had she waited too late to tell Cody how she felt?

Did he feel like he'd been rejected—as he must have every time he'd moved from one foster family to another?

That was probably why, even as an adult, that he had moved so often—not because it was habit, but out of self-preservation. He hadn't wanted to get attached to anyone or anything because every time he had—he'd had to leave it behind.

She should have told him how she felt about him. She should have made certain that he knew she loved him.

21

THE FIRE OUT WEST had been so dangerous that it had needed their entire focus. So Cody had been able to put off the discussion he needed to have with his team until they returned to Northern Lakes. Braden had told everyone that Cody was taking the smoke jumper position. There'd been no time to talk about it, though. Usually, in a fire like that, he only worried about his team—about Wyatt getting home to Fiona, about Dawson getting back to Avery.

Everyone else to their families. He wouldn't have worried about himself, or thought he had anything to return to—until now. Now he had everything: Serena.

And Stanley.

And even that damn dog.

He understood now how Dawson and Wyatt felt— why they were more antsy to get back than they were to leave. They were even more anxious now that they were close to home. But they'd respected his request to talk to them before they left the firehouse.

"You got us up here," Dawson said as he paced the third-floor conference room. After their two and a half weeks in hell, they should have been exhausted. But they were all restless—on edge. "What do you want?"

Braden uttered a ragged sigh as if he knew. But he had no idea—at least not the right one.

Cody drew in a deep breath, bracing himself before saying, "I want to stay."

There—he'd said it. The one thing he had always been too proud to say as a kid. Of course he'd known it wouldn't have mattered then. It had never mattered what he'd wanted. Nobody had cared. Until now...

Now he suspected otherwise. He felt it when he was working a line with the guys. He felt that they really cared about him, not just the work. They had more than his back. They had his heart.

"What?" Braden looked more shocked than he should have been since he'd known Cody had turned down the smoke jumper position.

"I want to stay on the team," he said. He stepped closer to his boss, and with his gaze steady, he added, "And it has nothing to do with the arsonist."

"You love us," Wyatt said, and he slung his arm around Cody's shoulders, squeezing him affectionately.

Cody squirmed away from Wyatt and hotly denied it. "No!" But he did.

And from their grins, it was obvious that they all knew it. Hopefully Serena knew it, too. Maybe that was why she had accused him of running away—because she knew he'd been too afraid to admit to his feelings.

"We're not the only ones you love, though," Wyatt said. "You love Serena, too."

He uttered the ragged sigh now. "Yes..."

And two and half weeks away from her—aching for her—had proved to him beyond any doubt that his feelings for her were real. And lasting. Now he just had to prove it to her.

Given the way he'd left, he doubted she would give him an easy time. He would have to work to prove it to her. But if it took him the rest of their lives to convince her, he wasn't giving up.

He wasn't giving up on *them*.

Dawson slapped his back. "That's great."

"Yeah," Braden agreed. "Let's go to the Filling Station and celebrate."

Wyatt and Dawson laughed like they used to when Cody had ignorantly suggested drinks upon returning to Northern Lakes after a long absence. He understood now why he had been the last person they'd wanted to spend any more time with after 24/7 shifts. Now he knew how badly they wanted—they *needed*—to be with the women they loved. And he joined in their laughter.

"Not now, boss," he said.

He had to get home to Serena. He had missed her too much. Hell, he'd even missed that house of hers. But before they could head out of the conference room, sirens blared.

Wyatt cursed as frustration overwhelmed him. "We just got back. We should let the volunteers handle this one."

But even before he heard the address of the fire, Cody knew where it was. This was why he hadn't wanted to leave Northern Lakes—because he'd known the arsonist was still out there, waiting to strike again. Waiting to hit him where it would hurt the most: Serena.

IT HAD BEEN so hot and dry again that the woods surrounding the house could catch fire, too.

Had Serena gotten Mrs. Gulliver and Mr. Stehouwer far enough away? Would they be safe where she had left them, leaning on each other, in the middle of the street? Her heart pounded with fear and concern.

Maybe help would come soon. She had called 911. They might arrive in time to help the older couple but not her other boarders.

"Stanley!" she cried out for the teenager as she headed up the steps to the front porch. Smoke rose from the house—burning through the hole in the roof where her quarters had once been. The attic was nearly gone now.

The fire must have started there. As she stepped inside, smoke billowed down the stairwell and sparks rained from the ceiling. The wires were burning inside the walls, spreading the fire even more. She ducked the glowing embers and coughed and sputtered.

But she couldn't leave—not without Stanley.

Mr. Tremont must not have been home when the fire started. His rental car wasn't in the circular driveway. But Stanley's old beater was. And when she'd been helping Mr. Stehouwer out, she had seen Stanley run back inside. She knew why when she heard the barking and the whimpering.

"Stanley!" she yelled. "Annie!"

The barking echoed down the stairwell. The dog had

to be on the floor above. And the frantic sound of her barking suggested she was trapped.

Since Cody had left, the boy and the dog were solely her responsibility now. She had to make sure they were all right. She had a cloth in her hand—the damp one she'd held over Mr. Stehouwer's face when she'd helped him from the house. He'd pressed it back into her hand when she'd left him. It was almost dry now. It wouldn't provide much protection. But she held it over her face as she headed up the steps.

The wood creaked ominously beneath her. So did the ceiling above her. She feared the whole house was about to collapse on top of her. Tears stung her eyes, but it wasn't just because of the smoke.

She was scared that she was about to die without ever telling Cody how much she loved him. She would have told Mrs. Gulliver or Mr. Stehouwer to let him know. But she had promised them that she would be right back—and that she would have Stanley and the dog with her.

A couple of weeks ago she had promised her sister that she wouldn't let the house kill her. But the house shuddered and creaked like it was about to implode.

Was Serena about to break her promises to everyone?

At least she hadn't made any promises to Cody— although she should have. She should have promised that she wouldn't be like all those other people who'd let him down.

She would never abandon or reject him, not on purpose. The step cracked beneath her weight, and her foot slipped through the hole. She pulled, but the splintered wood held tight. She was trapped in the burning house.

22

CODY'S HEART SHIFTED in his chest as he came upon the old couple standing in the middle of the street. They held each other tight. Their pale, wrinkled faces were smeared with soot.

He slowed the truck and asked them, "Are you okay?"

Mrs. Gulliver's usually perfect white-and-purple-and-pink hair was mussed and dirty. But he saw no blood on either senior citizen. He saw nothing but their shock and fear.

Through the open window of the truck, Mrs. Gulliver grabbed his arm. "They're in there, honey," she said. "They're trapped in that house."

He knew that; Serena wouldn't have left her elderly boarders standing alone in the road.

"The fire engine's coming," he assured them. He hadn't been able to wait for everyone else, though. The second he'd heard the address of the fire, he had jumped in the truck and taken off. "Help will be here soon."

Mrs. Gulliver squeezed his arm then slapped the side of the truck. "Go!" she yelled. "Save them!"

He pressed hard on the accelerator and raced down the driveway toward the house. The huge structure was fully engulfed, black smoke and flames rising from it. He threw open the driver's door and jumped out. As he raced up to the front door, the porch and the balcony above it collapsed. Flaming straw rained down around him. He'd already known but now he had proof: the arsonist had set the blaze.

He kept getting more and more dangerous. But he hadn't claimed a life yet. Cody wouldn't let him take one now; he wouldn't let him take anyone from Cody that he loved.

He hurried around the burning house to the back door that opened onto a brick patio. There were no shooting flames here. He pushed open the door and hurried inside the kitchen. Holes had burned through the tin ceiling, which was turning black; it was probably about to collapse like the porch.

Through the billowing smoke he found the back stairwell. The smoke was so thick—so pungent—he could barely see. But he forged ahead and stumbled onto the second-floor landing. A body lay on the floor, the curly mop of blond hair darkened with soot.

"Stanley!" he yelled. "Stanley!"

But the kid didn't move. A dog barked—it sounded rough and weak. Cody listened intently, trying to figure where the sound was coming from. Then he heard the scratching at the door behind him. Stanley had nearly gotten to Annie. Cody touched the wood; it wasn't hot—not like the rest of the structure, which was aglow with heat and fire. He turned the knob and pulled open the door. Annie—her usual boundless energy spent—crawled out, her head and body slouched low to the floor.

She licked Cody's face. Then she turned her attention to Stanley—drooling all over him. The kid swiped at her and murmured, "Go away…"

Cody gently slapped his face. "Come on, kid. Stay with me!"

Stanley's lashes fluttered and then his eyes opened. "Cody? You're home?"

He nodded. "Where's Serena?"

The kid's thin shoulders shrugged. "She got Mrs. G and Mr. S…" He started choking.

He'd inhaled too much smoke. Cody swung him over his shoulder and carried his limp body down the back stairs. Annie didn't come with him, though. He heard her feet scratching across the floor above as she headed down the hall toward the front stairwell.

That had to be where Serena was.

He dumped Stanley on the lawn outside—far enough from the house that if it collapsed, none of it would fall on him.

But what about Serena? Cody would lose her if he hadn't already. He hurried back inside but bypassed the kitchen stairwell. He could hear Annie barking near the front of the house.

So he hurried through the dining room. Holes burned through the coffered ceiling. The paneling turned black and curled away from the walls—leaving the wooden studs bare like the bones of a skeleton.

"Serena!" he yelled for her. But he had no hope that she could hear him. If she was conscious, she would have been with Stanley. She would have been rescuing him like she had her elderly boarders.

No. Serena was the one who needed saving now. He passed through the parlor and stepped into the foyer—what was left of it. The porch had collapsed on top of the chandelier, now lying in jagged fragments beneath it. Only a few steps were visible next to the banister.

She would be there, Cody knew, not just because he could hear Annie barking louder now. He knew it because he could feel that she was near but slipping away from him. He was running out of time if he didn't want to lose her forever.

So he held tightly to the banister as the steps gave way beneath him and he vaulted up, stepping over a gaping hole. The boards had splintered—from the heat and from someone kicking them. Serena must have been stuck. But she'd freed herself and she'd made it as far as the second-floor landing. She lay there, her black hair covering her face. Was she breathing?

A board must have struck her—it stretched across her back to the opening to the second-floor hallway. Annie pawed at it from the other side. Finally the dog's frantic efforts pushed it forward. Cody caught it before it struck Serena again. He shoved it behind him. Then he grabbed Serena. With Annie following on his heels, he ran down the second-floor hallway toward the back stairs. The ceiling and floor groaned above and beneath him, and as he ran, the house began to crumple in on itself.

The back stairs cracked under their combined weight as the heat destroyed the brittle wood. He slid down to the kitchen floor. Then he crawled toward the back door.

Later, he wasn't certain if he pushed open the door or if Annie did. He only remembered dragging Serena's limp body to where Stanley lay.

He didn't know if Serena and the kid were alive or if he'd lost them both. And in the distance, he finally heard the whine of the fire engine's siren. Help had arrived. But it was too late. The house was gone.

HER HEART POUNDING FRANTICALLY, Serena jerked awake with a scream. Or she would have screamed had her throat not been dry and burning. All she could manage was a whimper. Something cool passed over her lips and eased down her hurting throat.

"You're okay," a deep voice murmured, sounding nearly as hoarse as hers felt. "You're safe."

She opened her eyes and peered up at Cody. His beautiful green eyes glowed brightly in his soot-streaked face. Was she dreaming or dead? The last thing she remembered was rushing back into the burning house for Stanley and Annie.

Panic clutched her heart and she whispered, "Stanley…"

Cool fingers brushed across her cheek, wiping away tears she hadn't realized she was crying. Or maybe her eyes were just watering. Like her throat, they burned, too.

"He's fine," Cody said. "A little smoke inhalation. They're going to keep you both overnight to make sure your lungs aren't damaged."

"Mrs. Gul—"

"Mrs. G and Mr. Stehouwer are so healthy that the doctor didn't even want to keep them overnight. Tammy wanted to take them back to her place—probably to fix Mrs. G's hair—but there was an open room at the assisted living center in town." His eyes twinkled with humor. "They happily agreed to share it. The fire might have finally made them realize how they feel about each other."

She hadn't needed the fire to make her realize how much she loved Cody. She had loved him long before that. And she wanted to tell him.

But first she had to make certain everyone was fine.

"Annie?" She wasn't sure what Stanley would do if something had happened to that goofy pup.

"She's fine, too." Cody's lips curved into a faint grin. "Hell, she deserves a commendation for making sure everyone got out alive."

"So everyone's fine?" she asked, needing the assurance that no lives had been lost. "Everyone got out? Even Mr. Tremont?"

"Yeah," Cody replied. "Mr. Tremont had already packed up his stuff and was heading out of town."

She gasped. "You don't think…" She had checked him out, though. He had no criminal background. But maybe the arsonist didn't either. Maybe he was someone nobody would suspect.

He had to be, or they would have caught him before now.

"I did," Cody admitted. "I thought he could be the arsonist until I found out he works for Braden's ex's new husband. Or he did. He reported back to the guy that nothing was happening between Braden and Amy, so his assignment was over."

Now that she knew he was safe she didn't want to

talk about Mr. Tremont anymore. She didn't care about anything but Cody. "Why are you here?" she asked as she stared up into his face. He'd said he was never coming back to Northern Lakes.

"We'd just gotten back from the fires in California when the siren went off," he said.

That explained why the other Hotshots had returned, but not him. "But your other job…"

"What other job?" he asked. But his green eyes twinkled. He knew what she was talking about.

"That's not the job I want," he said.

"A new position came up?"

He nodded. "I hope so."

"Where is it?" she asked. Hopefully closer than Washington.

"Wherever you are." He leaned down and skimmed his mouth across hers, kissing her more tenderly than he'd ever kissed her. "Whatever you want me to be."

"Cody?" She must be dreaming because she couldn't understand what he was saying. His face was dark with soot and there was a slight scratch on his head. "Do you have another concussion?"

He chuckled. "No. I'm thinking more clearly than I have in a long time."

"I don't understand." She must have hit her head. "That smoke jumper job is all you've wanted. Stanley told me about the posters you used to have up in your room at the last foster house."

Cody shook his head. "Not anymore. That was a dream. But I realize now that what I really wanted was a family. A home. A place to belong," he said. "I found that with you."

She was afraid she'd lost all that, though. That the arsonist had taken it all.

"I love you," he said. "And I want to be with you."

The tears flowed now, and they weren't because of the smoke. Emotion overwhelmed her, because she knew nothing else mattered but this—but him. "I love you…"

He released a ragged breath of relief. "That's good."

How had he not known how she felt about him? Because nobody else had ever loved him. She should have told him weeks ago. She should have made certain he knew—in case something had happened to one of them.

"I'm sorry," she said.

He shook his head. "I'm the one who's sorry. I never should have left you."

"It's your job." And she would never keep him from that. "You had to go. You were needed to relieve those crews in California." She knew how important the Hotshots' jobs were.

"But I knew the arsonist was after me," Cody said. "I worried that he'd go after you if he really wanted to hurt me."

It made sense then that he would hurt her and Stanley and even the dog. Because no matter how much Cody had denied he cared, it was obvious that he did.

"Will you ever be able to forgive me?" he asked.

"For what?" He had done nothing wrong.

"For what you've lost," he said. He swallowed hard, as if choking on emotion as much as smoke. "The house is a complete loss. It burned to the ground. There's nothing left."

She'd already known that, but she released a shaky

breath. And his arms slid around her as he pulled her against his chest. His hands trembled as he stroked her hair.

"I'm sorry," he said—over and over again.

The breath she'd released had actually been one of relief. She didn't have to worry about the house anymore. With the insurance money, she could pay off Courtney and do whatever else she wanted with her half.

"That last day—as I watched you with Stanley I saw what a great foster home it would have made—what a great foster mom you would be."

The idea filled her with warmth and hope. "That's a great idea," she said.

"We'll rebuild on your property," he said. "We'll find old pictures of the house and replicate it. We will make it happen."

She shook her head. "Not now. Not yet…"

"Too soon?"

"Yes," she said. "It's too soon for me to settle down— to work so hard. I want to travel. I want to live a little." Like Courtney wanted her to live.

He touched her head now as if looking for bumps and bruises. "Are you okay?"

"I will be," she said. "As long as I can travel with you. If you want to reconsider and take that smoke jumper job, I will move to Washington with you. I'll go wherever you want to go."

He hesitated and she understood. He might love her, but he was used to being alone.

"Of course I know you'll be busy with training and everything," she assured him, hoping that she hadn't overwhelmed him, "so I don't have to go…"

"You don't have to go," Cody said, "because I'm not going. I turned down the job. I want to stay with the Huron Hotshots. We're family. And Northern Lakes is home."

Her heart swelled over the orphan, who'd never felt as if he'd belonged anywhere, finally finding his home. And love. "I love you."

"Do you love me enough to wait until the off-season to do that traveling?" he asked. "We can spend months exploring new places together."

She nodded. "It's a deal." They would have their adventure. But they would make Northern Lakes their home. And someday when they were ready to settle down completely, they would rebuild her house and make it the foster home Cody always should have had—the one filled with love.

* * * * *

Who is the Northern Lakes arsonist?
Sexy Hotshot boss Braden Zimmer joins up with a
beautiful arson investigator to bring the culprit to
justice in HOT PURSUIT,
the final story in Lisa Childs's
HOTSHOT HEROES series.
In stores January 2017.

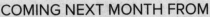

If the best way to get over someone is to get under someone else, handyman Chris Steffensen is definitely repairing Joey Silvia's broken heart. But is Joey's high school friend a guy she could really fall for?

Read on for a sneak peek from
HER HALLOWEEN TREAT, the first in a special holiday-themed trilogy from bestselling author Tiffany Reisz.

"I'm going to go up and see what he's doing." Joey saw a large green Ford pickup parked behind the house with the words *Lost Lake Painting and Contracting* on the side in black-and-gold letters.

"I'll stay on the line," Kira said. "If you think he's going to murder you, say, um, 'I'm on the phone with my best friend, Kira. She's a cop.' And if he's sexy and you want to bang him, just say, 'Nice weather we're having, isn't it?'"

"It's the Pacific Northwest. In October. It's forty-eight degrees out and raining."

"Just say it!

"Now, go check him out. Try not to get murdered."

Joey crept up the stairs and found they no longer squeaked like they used to. Someone had replaced the old stairs with beautiful reclaimed pine from the looks of it.

"Hello?"

"I'm in the master," the male voice answered.

Joey walked down the hallway to a partly open door.